Lovers & MADMEN

A Brothers *MALEDETTI* Romance

NICHOLE VAN

Fiorenza Publishing

Lovers and Madmen © 2021, 2018 by Nichole Van Valkenburgh
Cover design © Nichole Van Valkenburgh
Interior design © Nichole Van Valkenburgh

Published by Fiorenza Publishing
Print Edition v1.0

ISBN: 978-1-949863-09-3

To Dad—
For showing me every day the meaning
Of unconditional love, acceptance, and steadfast devotion.

To Dave—
For being my forever.

Lovers and madmen have such seething brains,
Such shaping fantasies, that apprehend
More than cool reason ever comprehends.
　　　—William Shakespeare, *A Midsummer Night's Dream*

I shall be telling this with a sigh
Somewhere ages and ages hence:
Two roads diverged in a wood, and I—
I took the one less traveled by,
And that has made all the difference.
　　　—Robert Frost

PROLOGUE

Would he do it?

Could he do it?

Knowing the end from the beginning as he did?

He watched as the woman laughed, head back, hair tumbling around her shoulders—a thick, curly mass of honey streaked with lighter gold.

She sat at a table with two other women, all three of them talking animatedly in the sidewalk cafe.

He had known she would be here today. All week, he had promised himself he would not meet her.

He would be content to love her only in the memory of possibility.

Besides, he knew most everything about her anyway. How much more was there to learn?

He knew, for example, she was American and had an undying love for animals.

He knew her eyes were vivid shades of blue and green . . . the Mediterranean Sea on a balmy summer day. He knew that her smile was wide and lush. That she was tall and curved in ways a man appreciates. That her voice had a husky, melodic edge and her nose crinkled when she was confused. That she preferred her coffee with plenty of cream and her pasta with extra sauce.

He did *not*, however, know her name.

And *that* desperate curiosity . . . in the end . . . was why he was here, leaning against a stone wall, staring across the piazza.

Did she have a flowy name that tripped off the tongue, like Savannah or Willow or Gabriella?

Or was her name more traditional, like Sarah or Rachel or Elizabeth?

Perhaps was it something unexpected, like Dulcinea or Imogen or Valeria?

And how could he live without knowing what to call her?

She haunted him, this woman.

He saw her in his dreams, a thousand scenes and only ever *her* that he loved. She brought him wild joy. A happiness that illuminated the bleak isolation of his life.

There would be no old age for him. Death would come long before gray hair. She deserved so much more from life than his broken self.

What if she knew? The thought whispered through him.

If she knew that blinding happiness *now* was irrevocably tied to horrific pain and grief *later*, would she still choose that future?

Would she still choose him?

And . . . could he walk away without even learning her name?

In the end, he wasn't sure he would have crossed the piazza. He might have remained on the knife's edge between seeing her and never physically meeting her, a boundary seemingly so innocuous but littered with endless future pain.

But she laughed again and leaned forward to listen to something her friend said, her hair catching in the wind and flying around her head in a halo.

She wrapped a hand around the mass, trying to tame it. Her movements were completely new to him, and yet, achingly familiar . . . as if he had already spent a lifetime watching her do the exact same thing.

In a way, he supposed he had.

As she wound her hair into a rope, her head turned. And like a compass seeking true north, her blue gaze snapped to his, locking him in place.

Electricity hummed through the air, hitching his breathing and kick-starting his heart.

She flashed him a flirty smile before turning back to her friends, again laughing.

But the damage was done.

His feet moved toward her without him consciously telling them to. He would just introduce himself, learn her name, give her an Italian *bacio* when he said goodbye—pressing his cheek to hers and kissing the air beside her ear, breathing her in—and then he would go.

He *had* to leave.

He loved her too much to keep her.

JUDITH CAMPBELL

FLORENCE, ITALY
JUNE, 1982

A man was staring at me.

Riveted. Unmoving. Watching.

Normally such staring would come off as creepy.

But as the guy was code-red, off the charts gorgeous, all my creepy-staring-cooties morphed into skittering goosebumps of attraction.

Why an attractive man got a pass on creepy behavior, I couldn't explain. Biology messing with my head, I supposed.

Just to be clear.

I didn't believe in romantic love . . . the intense, all-consuming emotion that Hollywood, Nashville and Broadway relentlessly promote.

I was a clear-sighted scientist and a doctor.

Love was nothing more than a fancy label for lust and emotional neediness, a potent mixture of genetics and physiology.

I was convinced capital-L *Love* was a marketing gimmick dreamed up by medieval French minstrels who then passed the idea down through the centuries until it had morphed into Disney fairy tales with anthropomorphic, talking animals and 'heroes' who kissed unconscious women because they were beautiful, but the men were handsome and rich and somehow that took the sexual assault of non-consenting women from, "Call the cops!" to "How romantic."

And, okay, maybe I got a little shouty and ranty about the subject from time to time. But I should have heeded that Bible verse about pride and falling.

My opinions about love shifted on a sweltering day during the first week of June.

I was in Florence, Italy with my two best friends—Kimberly and Sandra—for a goodbye-to-our-youth European fling. I had just finished grad school and would start my first grown-up job as a veterinarian in September.

Kimberly, Sandra and I were backpacking through Europe. We called it our Three-Three-Three Tour—three women, three months, thirteen countries. (The name had been Kimberly's idea; obviously math wasn't quite her thing—Art History major.)

I had left my boyfriend, Steve, behind in Portland, Oregon. Steve was in his second year of medical school and just as jaded on the concept of love as me. In fact, we had decided to take a 'break' while I was in Europe, mostly to give ourselves space to evaluate our relationship. I wasn't concerned about us falling apart; we were good friends and both too practical. We had even casually discussed marriage a few times, but we treated it as an event far in the future, once we were both fully established in our respective practices. I figured if I chose to get married, Steve with his similar interests and goals would make an excellent life partner. I wasn't madly, giddily in love with him but that was okay.

Love, after all, was a fallacy.

In hindsight, I realized that Steve was safe and convenient, and I took those emotions and decided, for me, that was 'love.'

But that was before I met *him*. And everything changed.

That morning, we three women were sitting sipping coffee at a sidewalk cafe in Piazza Santa Croce in central Florence, enjoying sunlight that verged on too warm and chatting about what we had on our agenda that day. We had just finished up our first week in Rome and were eager to continue exploring Italy.

Before leaving Portland, we had each made a list of three things (see above) that we wanted to do during our time in Europe.

Sandra wanted to drink coffee in three sidewalk cafes of every major city we visited because, "Coffee is such a ritual in Europe, but you can hardly find a European-style coffee-shop in the States. I'm telling you, there is a market for it here. I'm totally going to open one, and we'll sell espressos and lattes and stuff. It'll be huge. Like 'put one on every corner in America' huge. I'll call it something romantic like Starbreak or Barstruck. But first, I gotta do research."

Sandra maybe needed to lay off the caffeine.

But I did have her to thank for discovering *cremina*—an Italian concoction of sugar and cream that when mixed fifty-fifty with espresso made the most delicious morning wake-me-up. Add in some ice cubes with the summer heat, and I was in iced coffee heaven.

For my part of the trip, I wanted to see three scientific highlights in each country we visited. To that end, we had *Il Museo di Storia della Scienza*—the Museum of Science History—and its large display of artifacts related to Galileo on our list of things to see that day.

Kimberly's goal was to kiss three cute boys in each country.

So . . . yeah.

Again . . . Art History major.

Kimberly's kissing goal wasn't entirely unexpected as she was also the type who referred to all unmarried women as 'girls' and had 'game plans' for attracting 'boys.' Like romance was a winner-takes-all sporting event.

To be fair, Kimberly was also hilarious and loyal and a lot of fun, which explained our friendship. She made the best mix tapes and was always up for watching *M*A*S*H* (and sometimes **cough** *The Dukes of Hazard* **cough** because . . . John Schneider).

But that morning, Sandra was struggling to understand Kimberly's kissing goals.

"I just don't see how you're going to kiss that many men, Kimberly," Sandra said, leaning back in her chair and fanning her face with our guide map. "The math is against you."

Have I mentioned that Sandra had just graduated with an MBA in Finance?

"Math?" Kimberly said *math* as if it were any other crass, four-letter word. "What does *math* have to do with kissing?" Her blue eyes frowned and she slid her feathered, Heather Locklear haircut off one shoulder.

Sandra sighed. It was her chest-heaving, woe-is-me, Kimberly-is-a-blond-idiot sigh.

That sigh was rapidly becoming the soundtrack of our trip.

"Kimberly, we're visiting *thirteen* countries in twelve weeks," Sandra said the words slowly, as if that explained everything.

Kimberly blinked at her.

Sandra, again, sighed. "Three men per country . . . that's thirty-nine guys."

Kimberly blinked one more time. "I'm still not following how the math makes this a problem."

Sandra upped her sigh-ante to a growl. "Kimberly, how are you going to convince a whopping three point five guys a week to kiss you?"

Now it was Kimberly's turn to look affronted. Which, fair point, Kimberly's resemblance to Heather Locklear didn't stop at her hair—plainly put, she was stunning—but Sandra wasn't wrong about the math. Obviously, Kimberly hadn't thought through the kissing thing well enough.

"You do realize we're in Europe, right, Sandra?" Kimberly leaned forward, sweeping her hand in a circle to take in the piazza in front of us. "Getting a kiss from a European guy is as easy as breathing."

Sandra and I both stared at her.

"Allow me to educate you, as you two clearly don't get out enough." Kimberly huffed. "European men have this sexy, romantic vibe that American boys can't naturally carry off. American guys are always focused on themselves—*Look at these guns! Aren't I hot? You know you want me, babe.*" Kimberly did a shockingly good imitation of a flexing frat boy. "It's a total turn-off. But European men are all about the girl. They look into your eyes with fierce focus and, you just . . . know—" She paused, staring at me . . . fiercely. "—you're all they see. They have no problem telling you you're beautiful and gorgeous and perfect. It *should* feel weird and creepy, but somehow they simply make you feel valued and . . . *seen.*"

Mmmmm.

So maybe Kimberly *had* thought this through.

I struggled to decide if I was impressed or appalled.

Sandra shook her no-nonsense Princess Diana bob. "Romanticizing sexual harassment is not healthy, Kimberly."

Kimberly scowled. "You're just being judgy because I'm right. It's totally a European thing, Sandra. Case in point—that guy has been checking us out for over half an hour."

"What guy? Where?" Sandra turned in her seat, making a production of looking around the piazza. "Over there?" She pointed toward Santa Croce itself, the enormous medieval cathedral at one end of the large square. Obviously, subtlety and tact were not Sandra's fortes.

"Jeesh, Sandra." Kimberly pulled her back around. "That's not how you work this. No guy—European or American—wants to be with a girl who seems desperate. You have to play it cool." She nudged her head to the left, indicating the area behind her shoulder. "Over there, about eleven o'clock, just under the archway. Super hot Italian. Dark hair, black shirt with black pants."

The wind swirled my hair around my face, determined to strangle me. I made a production of wrangling my wildly curly hair over one shoulder and took the excuse to glance in that direction.

I spotted him instantly. My eyes snapped to his as if magnetized.

Capital H.O.T.

But he wasn't looking at *us.*

No. All his attention was razor-focused on *me.*

He leaned a shoulder into the stone column with casual elegance, hands jammed in his pockets, body exuding coiled strength. His hair was longish and carefully styled to look effortless. His clothing had the hang and drape that screamed 'money' as tastefully as possible.

More to the point, he was jaw-droppingly gorgeous. The kind of magnetism you read about and actors portray on the big screen but you assume doesn't actually exist.

This man proved otherwise.

Wow.

He was . . . stunning. Like seeing a mythical creature in the wild.

My heart sped up and I looked away. Just a single look at him made my skin ache from the inside, like all of me was itching to dash away and yet desperate to talk to him at the same time.

I swallowed and then laughed.

What an odd physical reaction to simply *seeing* a stranger.

Kimberly and her hunky-guy gushing must have rubbed off on me.

Sandra stole a glance and then looked back to us, giggling.

"He is *totally* checking us out, guys," she laughed.

Not us, I mentally amended. *Me. He's checking out me.*

Grinning, I wrapped my hair into a loose rope, surreptitiously ogling the Italian hunk in my peripheral vision.

A twinge of guilt threaded through me. I was supposed to be with Steve. He was still technically my boyfriend, even if we were on a 'break.'

But . . . looking didn't hurt, did it? It wasn't like I was going to fall madly in love with this guy, remain here in Florence, marry him and then birth four children in the span of as many years, right?

I mentally snorted. *As if.*

So I reserved my judgment even as Kimberly made a production of laughing and acting like we were having the time of our life.

The man was undeterred. Out of the corner of my eye, I watched him move across the piazza toward us. He had a smooth stride, confident and intent.

As he walked, I sensed that crazy magnetism again, like he and I existed in our own micro-climate that swirled with charged lightning.

The scientist in me found it two parts fascinating and one part appalling.

Why would my physical body have such an immediate adrenaline-and-pheromone-riddled reaction to a complete stranger? Why was evolution playing me like this?

He came closer and closer. Dodging the cars that zoomed around the exterior of the piazza, the gypsy children begging, the crushed masses of tourists pouring over maps.

Finally, I gave in to the lure of hormones and pheromones and genetics and brazenly turned my eyes back to his.

What would he do? Would he look away? Pretend not to notice?

The answer was immediate—

He would stare *straight* at me.

Our eyes instantly locked.

Electricity jolted me.

His dark eyes drilled into mine, plumbing my depths.

This time I didn't look away or lower my eyes. He held my gaze steady, a small smile tugging at his lips.

It *should* have seemed, at the very least, eccentric. But I somehow found it charming and sexy; he felt so safe and yet so very un-safe all at the same time. I was currently somewhere between hyperventilation and jubilation.

Clearly my fight-or-flight reflex needed some fine-tuning.

A hand waved in front of me. "Uh, earth to Judith?" Sandra snorted. "You okay?"

I nodded my head. At least, I think I did. I was too busy watching my Italian hunk close the remaining steps between us, my smile growing bigger the nearer he came.

He finally stopped directly in front of our table, eyes riveted on me.

Dimly, I noted Kimberly and Sandra swiveling their heads back and forth between Mr. Hunkaliscious and myself.

"*Ciao*," His husky Italian rolled down my spine with scorching intensity.

"Ciao," was all I managed to say around my abruptly thick tongue.

I gave my head a small shake. What was with this guy's charisma?

"Hi," Kimberly perked her head toward him and held out a hand. "I'm Kimberly."

His gaze shifted from me. I instantly felt released, both a relief and a loss.

"Cesare." He clasped her hand in his. He pronounced his name with a *ch* sound like Charles: CHEH-zah-ray.

Cesare.

Molto italiano.

Cesare then turned to Sandra who perkily offered her name and he repeated the hand shake.

And then the weight of his gaze was back on me.

No hesitation. No self-consciousness.

Just steady directness that said, *You fascinate me. You compel me.*

Damn Kimberly for being right.

I definitely felt . . . *seen.*

I bit my lower lip. His eyes darted downward, tracing my mouth in a lingering heated sweep, before coming back up to meet mine.

Annnnnnd . . . cue goosebumps.

My logical mind pointed out that this whole scenario should register code-red on my bizarre-o-meter.

Instead, it simply felt . . . familiar.

He felt familiar.

Oh, it's you, my heart whispered, sitting up. *There you are. I wondered where you'd gone.*

I shook my head.

Most certainly needed to nip unhelpful thoughts like that in the bud.

Logical. I was the logical, cool-headed one.

I had Steve waiting for me at home: steady, calm, easy-going Steve.

So this Cesare was good-looking.

So I wanted to plaster myself to him and spend an afternoon learning Italian from his *very* fine lips.

So what?

I sucked in a deep, fortifying breath.

"Judith," I said, extending my hand.

His warm palm engulfed mine, voltage zinging up my arm from the contact.

He didn't shake my hand. He didn't let go.

"Judith." He repeated my name in a breathy tone, briefly closing his eyes. Like just the *sound* of my name hurt him somehow.

He tugged on my hand, pulling me to my feet, reeling me closer to him.

Uhm, so maybe I would plaster myself to him after all.

I was tall—hovering just over five nine—but I was pleased to note he was even taller. Not by much, but enough, maybe just under six feet. Tall enough that my body hummed at the thought of being wrapped in his long arms.

Up close, his eyes were a complex hazel, not quite brown or green or gold but some in-between combo of all three.

I got lost in them.

He blinked and swallowed, clearly feeling our intense connection.

It had to be physical chemistry or homesickness or . . . or . . . *something*. My rational mind could not explain it.

He held my hand, trapped firmly between us.

"Judith." He repeated my name again with nearly sacred reverence. A prayer. A hosanna. "It is a pleasure to meet you—" A pause. "—*Judith*."

He leaned in and pressed his cheek to mine, kissing the air next to my ear. He pulled back and repeated the greeting on the opposite side, breathing in deeply as he did.

Never in my life have I been so completely physically aware of another human being—the scalding heat of his body, the rasping press of his whiskered cheek, the looming power in his shoulders, the scent of his cologne eddying pools of sandalwood and pine around me.

Chills chased my spine causing goosebumps to shudder along behind them. My breathing stuttered and my mouth dried up. Unconsciously, I canted toward him, all of me wanting more, more, more, until he consumed me and—

"Wowsa," Kimberly whispered behind me.

Her voice broke the trance. At least enough for me to take a step back, forcing Cesare to drop my hand.

I raised my eyes to his.

Yep. Still handsome. Still crazy attracted to him.

But my scientist self flooded forward, forcing me into clinical mode.

Logic. I did logic.

Okay, so I was physically attracted to a gorgeous, Italian guy who seemed to reciprocate some of that attraction?

Again . . . so what?

I didn't need to *do* anything about it. I could choose to act or not act. That was all.

Cesare smiled, slow and steady, looking as if he understood everything that had just passed through me. As if he had already spent a *lifetime* knowing me. Which, my scientist self rightly pointed out, was *absolutely impossible.*

Kimberly swiveled in her chair. "Care to join us, Cesare?" She waved a hand to the empty seat beside me.

Cesare paused, a frown briefly hitting his face. He stared at the chair, his expression almost . . . tormented. As if sitting in the chair was a serious decision, and he needed a moment to ponder all the ramifications.

Or maybe he was just worried about its stability. Italian cafe chairs were fairly dainty looking things.

I sat down in my own chair and wriggled a little in it. "I'm pretty sure the chair is safe. And we are all up-to-date on vaccines." I managed a small grin. "I promise I won't bite."

Cesare lifted his eyes back to mine. "*Peccato,*" he murmured.

I paused. Had he just said, *Too bad?*

But my comment seemed to have made the decision for him. In one swift motion, Cesare pulled out the chair and sat down, folding his wide shoulders and long legs into the smaller space.

"*Un caffè, per piacere,*" he called to a passing waiter, raising a finger in the air.

Kimberly grinned, salaciously meeting my gaze before turning to Cesare.

"So, Cesare," she began, "tell us about yourself. Are you a native of Florence?"

From that point, Kimberly launched into what I termed Interrogation Mode, asking question after question.

Cesare D'Angelo was my age, twenty-six. Single and not dating anyone. Never married.

He ran an art acquisitions business, D'Angelo Enterprises, that had offices a few streets over.

Studied at Yale in the U.S., which also explained his excellent English. Plus . . . Yale.

Though . . . Art Conservation major. Which meant he and Kimberly talked shop for ten minutes straight. (Not sure how I felt about his choice of major, honestly. Who wasted a degree from Yale on Art Conservation?)

Cesare was a native of Florence, where he currently lived above his business offices. *With his mother.*

"I love my mother," he deadpanned when I commented on that fact. "I am Italian. It's what we do."

During a lull in conversation, his gaze landed on the medallion I wore on a chain around my neck—a quarter-size disk with a crest of a lion on one side.

"May I?" he gestured toward it.

I nodded and leaned forward, placing it in his hand, shamelessly using the excuse to scoot closer to him. His cologne washed over me again.

He studied the front of the medal before turning it over.

"Judith Campbell. Presidential Scholar Gold Award for Innovation in Veterinary Medicine." He read the inscription on the other side. "Ah."

He dropped the medallion and sat back. "I did not know I was in the presence of a Gold Award winner." He said the words with a good-humored teasing edge, but a burn still climbed up my cheeks.

The medal had been a gift from my mentor, the only female faculty member in my program. Usually the winner got a plaque—and I had—but two weeks later, my mentor had surprised me with the medallion, too, saying she couldn't let, 'the first female winner of the award slip by without making more of a fuss.'

"Now I am intimidated." Cesare folded his arms across his chest.

"Because I'm a Gold Award winner?"

He nodded, smile popping up at the edges. "Not everyone gets a medal, I assume."

"True. Only those with Gold Award potential. Maybe next time." I patted his hand.

Cesare laughed. He had an amazing laugh, rich and deep.

We continued to talk about Florence and what we planned to do during our few days in the city.

And with every syllable out of his fine mouth, I fell a little more under his spell. I loved how his English flowed with the somewhat stilted cadence of a non-native speaker. How his words lilted at the edges with a gentle Italian accent, as if he couldn't help but add an extra vowel to the end of everything. How he spoke with his hands as much as his mouth—stereotypical but nonetheless true.

Of course, amidst all the liking and admiring I had going on, part of me was completely freaking out.

I knew *nothing* about this guy. Not really. He could be a serial killer. Or a mafia agent. Or, heaven forbid, a timeshare salesman.

But he charmed so effortlessly, I felt exhilarated instead of creeped out. It was the Italian way.

What's more, my heart vehemently insisted that he could be trusted. Which I logically noted was completely illogical, but whatever.

"So today you go the *Museo di Storia della Scienza*? Why have you chosen that over the Uffizi?" Cesare's tone clearly communicated how crazy he thought we were to *not* be visiting the enormous art museum housed in the sixteenth-century Medici office building.

"Well, Mr. Art History major—"

"Art Conservation," he instantly corrected me.

I wrinkled my nose. "There's a difference?"

His eyes narrowed but humor twitched his lips. "Funny."

"We're planning to visit the Uffizi tomorrow," I said. "But I got to choose for today, and I chose the science museum first."

"That is most illogical," he replied.

"I'm not sure you understand how logic works."

"Why would you not begin with the most celebrated museum in the city?"

"I suppose it depends on the criteria you use to categorize museums into phyla and genus."

A pause. Cesare's eyes lit up. "I categorize museums based on beauty."

"Ah. That is where we differ, you and I. I consider a museum's usefulness in informing human learning."

"Pondering usefulness seems . . . less exciting."

I shrugged. "Well, there is certainly more clothing involved in the scientific exhibits, so perhaps to some people, it *is* less exciting. And if you had one of these—" I held up my Gold Award medal. "—then you could win this argument, but until then . . ." I shrugged my shoulders.

"You are a cruel woman, Judith Campbell."

"I know."

"Well." He slapped his hands against his thighs. "There's no help for it. Now I have to come with you. We have a debate to settle."

"We do?"

"Of course. We must establish which is the better criterion—beauty or usefulness."

"Do they have to be mutually exclusive?" I asked, mostly to be bratty.

Cesare gave me a leisurely perusal—lips, throat, chest, hips, calves and then reversed back up—rendering my skin so very blazingly alive.

Whoa.

That had been just . . . *whoa.*

"No, *bella mia*, in your case, the relationship between beauty and usefulness is most definitely symbiotic. I could spend hours discussing how your beauty is most emphatically useful."

Mmmm, yes, please.

Cue me melting into a puddle of Cesare-induced goo.

Somehow, I managed to swallow and say through my tight throat:

"Well, what are we waiting for?"

2

"No, I disagree." Cesare pointed at the museum case, indicating the gold-leafed telescope inside. "He was a visionary."

"Galileo was a *scientist*, Cesare. Not some dreamer," I countered.

We were standing in the *Museo di Storia della Scienza*—a Renaissance-era building perched along the banks of the River Arno behind the Uffizi Gallery—staring at the telescope that Galileo Galilei had personally built and used.

Cesare and I had been bantering back and forth for the past two hours. Sandra and Kimberly had stuck with us initially but eventually moved on to the next floor of the museum, saying they would catch up in an hour once we had, "worked this weirdness out of our systems."

"You are trying to stuff Galileo into a box. Scientist. Dreamer." Cesare folded his arms, the motion stretching his shirt across his extra-fine shoulders. Were his biceps as strong as they looked? "He was both of those things. His visionary tendencies and imagination fueled his love of science. Your thinking is too binary."

Ugh.

This man.

Forget biceps. Why did his brain have to be even sexier than his brawn?

Didn't he know that man-smarts were like catnip for nerds? Was he deliberately trying to break the hearts of intellectual women everywhere?

Cesare continued, "In my opinion, cool logic and fiery creativity belong together."

"They *belong* together?"

"Yeah. They should probably get married." He said the words casually, but his eyes flicked to my lips as he spoke, sending a shock of skittering tingles down my spine.

Just.

Italian men.

I owed Kimberly a serious apology.

How was it possible I had only met him a couple hours ago? That aching sense of familiarity hadn't retreated. Instead, it had grown and flourished and flowered, sent down deep roots and taken up residence. Talking to Cesare was effortless and exhilarating and challenging and fascinating—

I stopped myself right there, giving my endorphin-laden self a solid shake.

What was I doing flirting and feeling giddy with a stranger when I had a perfectly respectable boyfriend at home?

I mentally frowned.

The feel-good parts of my brain didn't want to think about Steve right now. All my excited Cesare-intoxicated hormones steadfastly refused to board the Steve Guilt Train. So I was left at the station, perplexed that I *should* be on the Guilt Train, but mostly feeling guilty that I didn't feel guilty . . .

Where was I?

Right. Three hours deep into a Cesare-driven, hormone-drunk bender.

Blatant flirting aside, I refused to back down from my point.

"My thinking is hardly binary, Cesare," I retorted. "Portraying Galileo as a visionary poet-prophet instead of a serious scientist is ridiculous. That's just Victorian Romanticism talking, clouding history like it always does. You can't be sure Galileo was a dreamer. You can't *prove* it." I folded my arms to match his stance.

He *tsked*. "Science talking there. I wouldn't be so sure about what we can and cannot prove."

"Well, we can't know for sure the personalities and opinions of people long dead," was my brilliant comeback.

Cesare paused, eyebrow lifted, as if to say, *Perhaps I can.*

He had very nice eyebrows, dark and expressive, swooping with clean precision over his equally nice eyes.

"No. You're trying to get those eyebrows to win your argument." I pointed a finger at him.

"They can be very persuasive." He wiggled said eyebrows, a grin tugging at his lips.

My eyes flicked to his mouth. I had no doubt that other parts of his face could be extremely persuasive too.

"Nice try, buster, but you don't have one of these." I held aloft my gold award. "So sorry. You lose. Galileo was a rational scientist."

Cesare chuckled softly, looking at me like . . . I didn't know what. I wanted to say he looked at me like I was a feast after years of famine, like sunshine after a dark winter, and he was determined to savor every second in my company.

But Rational Me knew that thought had 'obsessive psychosis' written all over it.

"When you discount emotions as being irrelevant, you hamstring your ability to fully understand a situation or, in this case, a person. You introduce research bias."

"Feelings are the very *definition* of research bias, Cesare."

"I disagree. Just because something is not easily quantified and measured does not mean it is irrelevant or doesn't exist. It is simply more complex."

This exchange right here was why I was developing a mad crush on this man.

Not only was he brainy and razor sharp, but Cesare D'Angelo *liked* to match wits with me. He enjoyed arguing and making points and listening to my reasoning. He *wanted* me to be smarter and quicker with my replies.

This was a rare quality in anyone, man or woman.

I had spent most of my life pretending to be less intelligent than I was in casual conversation. Things were just easier that way. I didn't like it when my too-seeing brain and loud opinions and unnecessarily large words basically waved a banner screaming, 'This woman is Other! She's not like you!' Life was hard enough without me putting barriers between myself and the rest of the world.

That said, I had also spent years being one of the only women in a male-dominated, scientific field. I didn't shy away from confrontation when challenged.

But I knew from experience that most men didn't appreciate a woman showing off her smarts. Even Steve, easygoing and open-minded as he was, didn't like my 'professor mode' as he called it. Less kind men simply labeled me 'bossy' or worse.

But Cesare didn't seem to want the easier, more sanitized version of myself.

It was absurdly attractive.

Ugh.

Did he have to be hunky *and* intelligent *and* respectful?

I folded my arms, wrinkling my nose at him. "Science is science. Factual. Rational. Measurable. Emotions and things driven by emotion such as art and literature are by their nature subjective. They can't be measured or rationally studied. This makes them an unreliable source for obtaining information."

Cesare continued his keen staring, gaze going softer.

I saw it in that moment—the sadness that clung to him. A certain world-weariness. Melancholy, I'd label it. Like he had somehow seen too much and knew too much and it made him old before his time.

Though we were the same age, he felt a lot older. More wise. More grounded.

What had happened to give him such maturity?

His eyes skimmed over my face: eyes, nose, lips, chin, and then a brief stop on my lips again before coming back to my eyes. Cataloging. Assessing. As if carefully weighing what he would say next.

"What is the saying?" He cocked his head, thinking. "'There are more things in heaven and earth, Horatio,/Than are dreamt of in your philosophy.'"

"Shakespeare. *Hamlet.*" I named the source.

He nodded. "All I'm saying here . . . there is much you do not know, Judith Campbell. Do not discount that which is difficult to understand as *not* understandable." A pause. "Sometimes hard things are worth the effort. Just like Hamlet."

Something about his tone, the subtle emphasis he laid on the word *Hamlet*, had me looking at him. "Hamlet? Like understanding the play?"

"That, too."

I stopped, my face a question mark. I pursed my lips. His words had layers, and I got the sense he was hinting at something. But what?

Sometimes hard things are worth the effort. Just like Hamlet.

What did Cesare mean by that? Was he referring to something else?

The only other Hamlet that jumped to my mind was my childhood cat, Hamlet. When I was eleven years old, I had found him in a shed behind our house, a tiny, malnourished kitten. I had nursed him for weeks—waking around the clock to feed him—carefully coaxing him back to health. It had been exhausting work, but so rewarding. Basically, worth the effort. Hamlet was the reason I had decided to become a veterinarian.

But, that wasn't what Cesare meant, of course. There was no way he could know about Hamlet. I doubted even Sandra or Kimberly knew about Hamlet the Cat. It wasn't something that came up in casual conversation.

The moment slid past and I chalked it up to a weird coincidence.

We finished our walk through the museum and gift shop, moving on to other topics. Cesare, for all his talk of art and emotions and feelings, knew a staggering amount about Galileo and early scientific discoveries in general.

It was crazy sexy.

Kimberly and Sandra were standing just outside the exit to the museum gift shop, having spent the last hour flirting with guys passing on the street. Cesare and I waved a hand at them before crossing the busy road to the sidewalk opposite and its sweeping view of the River Arno. The Ponte Vecchio sat to our right, its distinctive medieval houses cantilevered over the water. We both rested our elbows on the stone wall overlooking the river.

Cesare had circled back to our earlier discussion. "You say that emotions are unmeasurable—"

"Because it's true."

"—but if something is unquantifiable, then how do you know emotional things?"

"What do you mean?"

"How do you know you love, for example?" he asked.

"How do I know I love—"

"Who does Judith love?" Kimberly's voice at my elbow caused me to jump.

I turned to her, giving Cesare my shoulder.

"Wait, Judith's in love with Cesare? Already?" Sandra joined her, not catching all our conversation.

A scalding blush flashed over me. "No!"

I swore I heard Cesare say, "*Peccato*" again behind me, but that would be insane, so I ignored it.

I shot my friends a wide-eyed, *shut-the-hell-up* look. I turned back to Cesare with a forced laugh.

Fortunately, he had an amused expression on his face.

"Ignore them." Time enough to kill my friends later. "You were saying?"

Cesare opened his mouth to continue.

And then Sandra's clueless voice sounded behind me, talking to Kimberly: "I thought Judith was in love with Steve."

I was staring right into Cesare's eyes when her words reached him.

In the moment, I don't know how I expected him to react. Confusion? A strained smile?

Instead, he flinched and something like betrayal flitted across his face.

"You're in love? With . . . Steve?" he asked, his brows drawing down, voice strained. "Who's . . . *Steve?*"

Silence.

My mind floundered.

"He's her sorta boyfriend." Sandra again.

She was so dead to me.

Cesare's head went back. "How did I not know about Steve?"

"Uh . . . because I didn't tell you?" It came out a question. "I guess we hadn't reached the discuss-other-relationships-in-detail part of our conversation?"

Why was Cesare reacting like this? Yes, we had some off-the-charts chemistry, and my brain had made out with his brain as we talked, but we were barely more than strangers. How was he supposed to have known about Steve?

Kimberly, bless her, instantly caught on to the vibe.

"Sandra and I are going to go get some gelato," she said.

I turned around and Kimberly pointed down the street.

"We'll wait there for you. Let you . . . uh . . . sort this out." She shot a glance behind me at Cesare.

"I'm sorry, Judith," Sandra whispered, looking stricken.

I watched them walk off, taking a moment to collect my thoughts, keenly aware of Cesare behind me, staring ahead.

My strong emotional reaction to Cesare was at once terrifying and exhilarating. We had talked effortlessly for hours over the course of the day, bouncing from topic to topic, never tiring. I couldn't remember ever clicking with someone so quickly.

But . . .

I was just starting a three-month long trip, Florence being one of many stops. I had Steve at home, even if we were 'on a break.'

Cesare and I were ships passing in the night.

So with that thought firmly in my mind, I turned, expecting him to be gazing at me with more of that puzzling betrayal. Instead, I found his eyes fixed on the Ponte Vecchio, almost unseeing.

Wind tugged at his clothing, pulling his shirt tight across his shoulders, outlining his well-defined musculature.

"Cesare?" I touched his arm.

He continued to stare at the bridge.

What was Cesare seeing?

I leaned over the wall, studying the sluggish water as it passed under the wide bridge.

It all looked normal to me. The River Arno flowed down a wide channel that was lined with enormous stone blocks to keep the water corralled and minimize flooding.

"Cesare?" I asked again, louder this time.

He abruptly lurched to life, turning to me. Huh. He simply must not have heard me before.

"Your friends all set?" he asked, his expression pensive, nothing more. All his emotions had gone on lock down. That same breeze ruffled his hair.

"Yeah. I'm going to meet up with them in five minutes." I waved a hand down the street.

I swallowed, unsure what to do. I extended a hand toward him.

"Thanks for an amazing day." Even to my own ears, the words sounded lame and fake.

"Yes." He looked at my hand for a second before trapping it between both of his.

He had nice hands, slender fingers, broad palms, defined wrists, a smattering of dark hair against his skin.

I had to clear the air on one point. I couldn't leave letting Cesare think I was the kind of woman who would flirt with one man while being in a relationship with another.

"So . . . Steve . . ." I began.

"Your boyfriend."

"Yeah . . ." I blew out a puff of air. "It's like this. Yes, Steve has been my boyfriend for a while, but we agreed to a break when I left for this trip."

He continued to study our joined hands as I spoke, not raising his gaze back to mine.

Turning my hand over, he traced a finger across my palm.

I resisted a shiver.

A single fingertip should *not* be so thrilling.

"A break?" he prompted.

"Like . . . it's okay for us to flirt with other people and be . . . open to other options, I guess. Basically, Steve and I are taking a step back from the relationship for a couple months."

Cesare's head snapped upright. "But how could a man who loves you want to be apart for an entire summer? And if you love this man, why take a . . . *break* while you're here in Europe?"

"I never said I was in love with him." I huffed again, tugging my hand free from his grasp. His hand voodoo was sousing up my hormones again. "Like I've been saying, Cesare, I don't think romantic love is actually a thing."

Cesare stilled.

I had been saying similar variations of the idea all afternoon, but even as the words left my mouth, they felt hollow. I didn't actually believe that love was a fallacy, not for everyone else.

Just for me.

He motioned between us. "Do you want this to be goodbye?"

I sank into his gaze, hazel and soulful.

Words crowded my throat, tangling my tongue. Something constricted my chest, making breathing difficult.

No. No I wasn't sure I wanted to say goodbye. Not yet.

"What are you doing tomorrow? The Uffizi, you said?" he continued.

"Yeah."

"Ah." A small smile appeared. "Feeling, then."

My smile matched his. "Yes."

A beat.

"Let me join you." His words tumbled between us.

I wanted to spend more time with him. The ache of it nearly suffocated me. A thousand thoughts winged through my brain, but I felt incapable of holding them. My heart fluttered in my throat.

Stupid feelings hijacking all my logic.

He misread my hesitation.

"I understand that you have your Steve at home, even if you are on a break. I will respect that."

"Oh, well, it's not—"

"Let us enjoy being together on our own terms." His eyes warmed. "You are an exquisite woman. Let me be an Italian man."

Uhmm.

Wow.

Okay.

Yes.

Please.

Let'sdothat.

He continued, "And thirty years from now after a life with your Steve, you can look back on me as . . . as a beautiful memory."

I sensed melancholy in his tone, but I didn't understand it either, so I simply replied: "Okay."

His smile grew, wide and delighted.

"Thank you, Judith Campbell. I will join you at the Uffizi tomorrow."

"You can just call me Jude, if you want. You don't have to say my whole name."

"But I like saying Judith Campbell. It is new to me, so I savor it." Again, I sensed layers in his words but couldn't figure them out.

We chatted logistics and then he tugged me closer for a very Italian cheek press/air kiss goodbye.

"*Ciao, bella. A domani.*"

'Til tomorrow.

I watched him walk away.

And given how much swagger he put into his saunter, I'm pretty sure he felt my eyes boring a hole in his shoulder blades.

3

"So why are we here again?" Kimberly asked.

Sandra rolled her eyes. "We've been over this, Kimberly. We're just doing a little fact checking."

Kimberly glanced at me and then back at the storefront across the street.

After leaving Cesare, we had eaten dinner at a pizzeria before heading toward our hostel. Sandra had, correctly, pointed out that we should at least check out Cesare's story as much as possible before meeting him at the Uffizi tomorrow. Just being street smart. Even though I instinctively trusted him, we hardly knew him. Cesare D'Angelo was barely more than a stranger.

Of course, I countered, hanging out with him in a public museum tomorrow would be safe enough, right? I would have my friends, and

I was big on the buddy system. My mom had a twin sister, so she was emphatic that everyone have a buddy with them at all times.

But Sandra was adamant that we be smart about this.

"We want to keep Judith safe," she said.

"I thought we wanted Judith to get kissed," Kimberly replied.

"No, that's your goal, not mine," I clarified for her.

"It's any red-blooded girl's goal, Jude. Get with the '80s here," Kimberly shot back.

"I have Steve," I grumbled, mostly because I felt like I had to.

"No, you don't." Kimberly wagged a finger at me. "You're on a break, so that excuse doesn't work."

Should I feel guilty about hanging out with another man? How would I react if I found out Steve had met some cute cheerleader type and flirted with her?

Hmmmm.

I searched my emotions. As usual when thinking about Steve, they gave me little.

Logic, however, supplied that Steve and I were on a break and if Steve wanted to hang out and watch *Solid Gold* with a bleached blond airhead, that was his prerogative. I supported him in his decisions.

I definitely didn't feel jealous or sad at the thought.

Logic and Emotion found that . . . interesting.

"Nothing is going to happen with Cesare," I said.

"Well, clearly nothing long term, duh." Kimberly rolled her eyes.

"What's that supposed to mean? You don't think I'm good enough for him?"

Kimberly looked perplexed. "It's not that at all, Jude. If anything, it's the opposite. But you're missing the point. European men love flirting with tourists because we're safe."

"Safe?"

"Yeah, they can shamelessly flirt and be outrageous and suffer no real consequences, because we'll be packed up and gone in the morning, off to the next city, the next guy. It's like the whole point of a European vacation."

"Oh." Hadn't Cesare said essentially the same thing?

A beautiful memory, he said.

Why did that thought make my chest hurt?

"Enough, you two." Sandra interrupted. "Cesare clearly has the hots for Judith. We're just making sure the basics he told us check out."

"Well, he's obviously legit." Kimberly flicked her hand, indicating the building across the way.

A glass storefront stood at ground level with the words *D'Angelo Enterprises* engraved on it. The building was located exactly where Cesare said it would be, nestled between orange and yellow apartment buildings along a quiet Florentine side-street. A large, arched passageway sat to the left of the storefront, running underneath the building to what looked like a courtyard behind.

Evening sun streamed down the road, casting long shadows. We were only two weeks off the summer solstice, so the sun wasn't setting until nearly ten o'clock.

Sandra sighed. "Okay, so the building is here, sure," she conceded, "but that doesn't mean that Cesare actually lives here. He could have just said this was his business."

"Or, more likely, he's totally on the up and up," Kimberly snorted. "You've been reading too many old-school Agatha Christie novels, Sandra."

"I don't see how that factors in here."

"You're paranoid, duh?!"

Sometimes I worried it was going to be a long three months with these two.

"Cesare is legit, the real-deal," Kimberly continued. "He's going to marry Judith, and they're going to have cute little Italian-American babies and name me as godmother so I'll have an excuse to come visit them in Italy whenever I want."

Sandra and I both turned to stare at Kimberly.

"You . . . uh . . . you've really thought this through, haven't you?" I managed to say, my voice a little squeaky.

I wasn't sure if I was reacting to her quick escalation of my after-noon flirtation with Cesare, or if I liked her rundown of my possible life plan a little too much.

Babies with Cesare? Cute, little dark-haired kids running around, chattering away in Italian and English—

Oof.

My ovaries nearly exploded at the thought.

"So we're here. We've established that this much of Cesare's story is true. Should we go ring the bell? Ask to meet his mom?" Kimberly's voice was sarcastic, but Sandra and I looked at each other.

It wasn't such a terrible idea.

But before I could say anything, the sound of keys in a lock jangled down the street, coming from the arched passageway next to the D'Angelo storefront. We instinctively pulled back into the doorway where we stood, hiding in the evening shadows.

A tall, familiar figure stepped out of a door in the passageway and turned onto the street, back to us, walking away in a hurry. He adjusted something draped over his shoulder as he moved.

Cesare.

"Okay, well," Sandra whispered, watching him walk away. "I will take that as proof that he lives there."

Kimberly and I nodded.

"So . . . anyone else wonder where he's going?" Kimberly asked.

"And why he has a massive coil of rope slung over his shoulder?" Sandra added.

"Yeeeeeah," I said, dragging out the word.

It was . . . odd.

"No way we're not following him on this one, ladies," Sandra took off after Cesare. "I'll have nightmares wondering otherwise."

We fell into step, keeping half a block behind Cesare.

What else we were supposed to do?

"We should run and overtake him," Kimberly suggested. "Act like we just happened to see him again and ask about the rope."

"We could, but then we'd never know what he intended to do with that rope. Sure, he could tell us, but we wouldn't know if it's the truth," Sandra replied.

"I'm with Sandra on this one," I said. "If I'm spending the day with the guy tomorrow, I would like to know what he was out doing the night before with a hundred feet of thick rope."

"It's not like there's a rocky cliff face around here to climb or cattle to hog-tie," Sandra said. "I don't know what else you'd use rope like that for. At least, no legitimate purpose."

I agreed, chewing on my lip.

What was Cesare up to? His movements were sure and quick. He was clearly determined to reach a specific destination as quickly as possible.

To say that this situation was outside my frame of reference would be an understatement.

My life up to this point had consisted of rational choices. I had been raised by loving, supportive parents who encouraged me to carefully examine decisions before making them. Rash behavior almost always resulted in painful, messy consequences.

But less than twelve hours in with Cesare, and here I was stalking a man through an ancient European city—a man I hoped to spend more time getting to know. I felt like I had tumbled down a rabbit hole into topsy-turvy land where strangers were best friends and logic got the heave-ho.

We tailed him up the road, across a busier avenue and into the more crowded, pedestrian streets in central Florence. Cesare appeared to be heading generally north, staying a block or two east of the River Arno. He moved with long-limbed grace, feet eating up the pavement.

We decided if he saw us, we would pretend that we had just seen him. It would be that simple.

But . . . he didn't look back.

After about ten minutes of walking, Cesare loped into the enormous Piazza della Signoria, the administrative heart of the city. The medieval city hall, the Palazzo Vecchio, stood to one side. A replica of Michelangelo's *David* towered to the left of the main entrance, situated where the original had been for hundreds of years.

Cesare didn't stop or hesitate, weaving his way through the gathered crowds of tourists and street sellers. We managed to follow, if only barely. It helped that I was tall, allowing me to track him over the crowds.

He crossed the piazza and moved down the wide avenue opposite the Palazzo Vecchio.

"Where is he going?" Sandra kept asking.

"Yeah. He's moving deeper and deeper into the city, not out of it," I added.

"Exactly. And he's clearly going in a hurry."

"Like he's late for something."

"Maybe he has to work on his knot-tying merit badge?" Kimberly offered.

Cesare went a block up the wider avenue before turning left onto another major road. Dodging taxis and people, we followed.

A hundred yards later, we crossed the road that ran alongside the River Arno and walked onto the Ponte Vecchio, still half a city block behind Cesare. Jewelry shops lined the bridge, but an arched loggia stood in the center, framing an expansive view of the city and its surrounding hills, awash in the reds and oranges of sunset. Tourists crowded into the loggia, snapping photos of the river turned to molten gold in the fading light.

Cesare shouldered his way through the people with almost brutal intent, pulling the rope off his arm as he went.

"What the hell?" Sandra hissed.

We pushed our way through the crowd too, trying to see exactly where Cesare had gone.

I pulled up to the railing just in time to watch Cesare finish tying one end of the rope to the stone balustrade. The rope was knotted about every two feet, something I hadn't noticed with it coiled. Cesare then climbed over the stone railing, wrapping a hand around the rope, nothing else between himself and a free-fall into the wide river below.

"Okay," Kimberly said in my ear. "So . . . recreational bridge dangling?"

"I think the new-fangled word for that is bungee jumping," Sandra clarified. "I read a news article about it. These guys from Oxford tied elasticized ropes around their ankles and threw themselves off some bridge in Bristol—"

Kimberly rolled her eyes. "I'm not sure—"

"AHHH!!" A woman in the crowd screamed.

Heads turned toward the sound.

More people screamed, shouting in foreign languages, pointing and pushing forward, crowding us against the railing.

I bopped up on my tiptoes, trying to see what was going on.

"A child!" A man yelled in English. "There's a little kid in the river."

"Someone help!"

"*Aiuto!*"

I scanned the river. Sure enough, a small child bobbed along in the current, head barely above the water, flailing and struggling.

My heart lurched.

I looked side-to-side, trying to see if there was a way down, which is when I realized the obvious.

Cesare was already descending toward the water, climbing down his rope, using the knots to aid his feet and hands. People screamed at him, pointing at the child.

Cesare nodded and twisted around, keeping the kid in his sight as he continued to rapidly descend. His arms flexed and corded with the strain, muscle bulging.

"Thank goodness he's here," someone yelled.

People continued to call down to Cesare. But he wasn't hearing them. He was one hundred percent focused on the little kid. Reaching the water, Cesare waited for just seconds. The child bobbed closer and closer, frantically paddling toward Cesare.

My heart choked me, pounding in my throat. Would Cesare reach the kid in time?

The current swirled once, twice, curling around the enormous stone pillars driven deep into the river bed, threatening to pull the child out of Cesare's reach.

But Cesare leaned heavily to the side, causing the rope to swing. Using the momentum, Cesare swung over the child at the last minute, looping an arm around the kid's chest, pulling him spluttering out of the water.

The crowd erupted in cheers. Several men grabbed onto Cesare's rope, pulling it up, one knot at a time.

"What a miracle!"

"What are the chances he had a rope right here?"

But I already knew—

Cesare had come here on purpose. He had left his house over twenty minutes ago with a rope over his shoulder and urgency in his gait.

It was no coincidence.

How?

How had he known that a child would be in the water right now? How had he timed it so perfectly? Had someone called him and told him? Had this been planned?

I stared at the child clinging to Cesare's neck. The kid couldn't be any older than five or six. No way the little guy would have survived that long in the water, right?

And why call Cesare instead of the police?

My mind reeled with questions.

The crowd surged forward, hands reaching to pull Cesare and the kid over the railing. Police sirens wailed. Sandra, Kimberly and I moved back from the stone railing and into the recess of a worn door, wood dark with age.

"Now what?" Sandra murmured in my ear. "Should we leave?"

I shook my head.

I had too many questions rattling through my brain, too bewildered to understand what I had clearly just seen.

The police arrived in force, followed by an ambulance. The child's frantic parents weren't far behind, talking hysterically in what sounded like German, as they wept over their child.

So . . . probably not a set-up.

Cesare was a hero. A brave Good Samaritan who had been in the right place at the right time.

But, again, . . . how? How had he known the child would be in the water?

My logical brain knew that the odds of this being a coincidence were astronomically high.

But any other explanation was . . . impossible.

Maybe Cesare habitually dangled from his rope, just in case?

Even I knew that sounded lame.

The police began shooing people away, cordoning off the scene.

The crowd parted enough for me to see Cesare, head bowed, talking to an officer, chest still heaving from the exertion. The front of his shirt was plastered to his pectorals and abs, every muscle defined.

As if feeling the weight of my gaze, he raised his head, eyes instantly locking with mine.

Connection. Electricity. Awareness.

My breathing snagged, tight and aching in my chest.

This is irrational, the logical part of me hissed. *You can't get hung up on someone so quickly. It just doesn't make sense.*

I couldn't look away; he held me fast.

You are an exquisite woman. Let me be an Italian man.

Cesare was a potent siren call.

Without thinking, I took several steps toward him.

An arm stretched in front of me, stopping my forward momentum.

I looked down at a shorter Italian officer. He said something in rapid-fire, staccato Italian, gesturing toward the sidewalk behind me.

I glanced back to Cesare, but he had turned his head, responding to more questions.

The officer repeated the same phrase, this time more emphatic.

Right.

I stepped back.

"C'mon, lover girl. He's gonna be wrapped up for a while. You'll see him tomorrow and we can get the lowdown on this." Sandra placed a firm hand under my elbow.

I allowed myself to be swept away in the tide of humanity walking away from the scene. But that didn't stop me from turning my head and staring at Cesare until he vanished from view.

4

We stayed up late that night, talking about the river incident. It was just . . . bizarre.

How had Cesare known?

Of course, Kimberly and Sandra spent a solid two hours dissecting every little bit of our interaction with him. Honestly, it was a level of obsession I didn't quite understand, though if any man were to drive me to it, I supposed it *would* be Cesare D'Angelo.

Worse, there was no way to know his history. We most certainly didn't speak enough Italian to research public records at the local library, assuming that was even possible in Italy.

But a man who would pull a child out of a river at his own personal risk couldn't be all that bad of a person, right?

I lay awake after our discussion, parsing through the day. My conclusions:

One, Cesare's pheromones acted as a stimulant for my own. In other words, we were animal attraction and natural selection at work.

Two, the sense of connection I felt to him was most definitely a by-product of number one (see above).

Three, I was a grown adult woman and if I wanted to indulge in a hot flirtation with a gorgeous Italian guy, then I was allowed to make that choice.

Four, it was imperative I remember conclusions one and two when in the midst of conclusion three.

Besides, surely today had been simply a one-off day with Cesare. Chances were I'd meet him tomorrow and feel nothing.

That was that last thought I had before falling asleep.

TRUE TO HIS WORD, THE next day we found Cesare waiting for us under the Loggia dei Lanzi opposite the entrance to the Uffizi museum.

He was gazing the other way as we approached, so I stared in shameless, brazen evaluation. Cesare was casual and relaxed in slacks with a loose white button-down shirt open at the throat and cuffed at the wrists. His hair was slightly more tamed today, but only barely.

He looked scrumptious. My hormones were more than ready for round two of a Cesare-kegger.

So . . . strike one on the physical attraction being a fluke. Definitely a thing.

And then, like the night before, Cesare whipped his head around, as if sensing the weight of my gaze.

His eyes immediately locked to mine. Electricity zapped my spine.

Annnnd strike two . . . that crazy sense of connection was so very real.

His smile grew wider and wider the closer I came, his gaze devouring me, as if he could scarcely believe that I was here and this was happening.

He greeted me just as he had the day before, a lingering kiss on each cheek.

"*Ciao, bellissima.*" His bass rumbled in my ear.

He pulled back, surveying me from head-to-toe. As it was a decidedly masculine perusal, his scrutiny lit a scorching path along my body.

"I'm glad you're doing okay today," I smiled. "I couldn't believe last night. You were quite the hero, saving that kid."

We had decided to not mention that we had been following him. Cesare didn't need to consider us stalkers.

But I most certainly wanted to hear his explanation.

He shrugged. "It was nothing, really. Just happened to be in the right place at the right time."

"Talk about a coincidence, though." Sandra jumped into the conversation.

"Yeah, it was good luck," was all he said.

"It was crazy you were there with a rope like that," Kimberly added.

"In the middle of Florence," Sandra chimed in.

"It happens sometimes." He shrugged. "I like rope."

Cesare's expression was inscrutable. I got no read off him. Why couldn't his face be scrutable? I wanted a better answer.

Grrr.

"Are you ready to see the Uffizi?" Cesare changed the subject. "Today is your last full day in Florence, isn't it?"

"That's the plan," I said.

"Yes," Sandra said.

"It is?" That was Kimberly. She turned to me, confused. "I thought we were just playing things by ear."

Yeah. It was going to be a long summer.

Cesare looked back and forth between us, eyebrows raised, mouth amused.

"Our schedule is . . . fluid." I replied to his unspoken question. "But this morning is the Uffizi and then we'll make decisions later."

Today *was* supposed to be our last full day in Florence. We had thought to hop the train to Venice tomorrow, though I hadn't lied when I said we weren't on a precise timeline.

A huge part of me was desperately sad to leave Cesare, our intense connection severed just as I started to explore it. Like having the smallest taste of a decadent dessert before pushing it away.

But I couldn't stay; that was absurd. And a long-distance relationship was fraught.

So that left here and now.

A beautiful memory.

I surveyed the ticket line stretching across the Piazza della Signoria.

Kimberly followed my gaze. "We're going to be waiting for hours to get in."

"That's fine," I said. "Cesare can tell us about his rope habits."

Cesare shot me a quick look, before clapping his hands together. "Never fear, my new friends. I have resources."

"More rope?" I asked.

Cesare chuckled. "Come."

He beckoned us across the street and down the small road between the Palazzo Vecchio and the Uffizi. He knocked on a recessed door just around the corner from the main museum entrance. A middle-aged woman, dressed in a stylishly professional suit jacket and matching skirt, pushed the door open.

Cesare chatted with her in Italian, laughing easily and leaning in to greet her with the typical *baci* on each cheek.

The woman smiled and then waved us inside.

When I hesitated, Cesare pressed a hand into the small of my back. "This is Enza," he murmured in my ear. "She's a business associate and agreed to slip us into the museum ahead of the queue."

"Wow. Thanks. You are a man of endless resources."

"You have no idea."

"Well, I have some. Rope and now this."

"I'm taking that as a compliment."

"I'd like to know more about your resourcefulness."

"All in good time."

What did he mean by *that?*

Cesare applied pressure to the small of my back, urging me forward. Enza smiled and led us through a series of offices to a side gallery of the museum proper.

"Enjoy the museum," were her parting words before shooing us into the gallery and closing the door to the office space.

Kimberly was beside herself with glee. "Oh my gosh, is that a Botticelli?" And she was off.

"Thanks for getting us in, Cesare," Sandra said to him before shooting me an apologetic look. I already knew she would be off with Kimberly.

So much for the buddy system.

Thirty seconds later, it was just Cesare and I staring at each other as tourists eddied around us.

I took a step closer to him. "Seriously, Cesare. About the rope. How did you know? It just seems . . . crazy."

Was it my imagination, or did he flinch slightly at the word *crazy?*

But I needed an answer. It felt vital.

Cesare stared into my eyes, expression clouded. "I can't explain it to you, *cara*. I simply had a feeling."

"A feeling? Seriously?" I almost rolled my eyes, half turning away from him.

"No, please don't." He stopped me with a gentle hand to my arm. "It *was* a feeling, and because of that, a child's life was saved. I can't say more. You're just going to have to trust me."

Trust.

The word hung between us, laden with . . . what?

Promise? Change?

My heart, emotions and body screamed at me to nod my head, trust him and never look back. They were all on-board with getting to know Cesare up close and personal.

But my logical brain overrode them.

Patience, grasshopper.

Logical me pointed out that such an immediate sense of trust was *not* to be trusted. I had barely known this guy twenty-four hours.

And given that Cesare would be moving from 'present' to 'memory' in another twenty-four hours, worrying about any of this was moot.

Cesare stepped even closer to me, murmuring in my ear. "You are conflicted, *cara*, because things happen that you cannot explain away. It's okay. You don't have to understand everything. Let us simply have an enjoyable day."

I adored how his words lilted at the end, his vowels a little too pure, his cadence somewhat stilted. The warmth of his breath circled around my senses, urging me to lean into him, soaking up the delicious headiness of his company.

"Okay," I finally managed to whisper in reply.

"Excellent," he said, wrapping a hand around mine. "Come. There is something I want to show you."

He led me down a corridor and through several rooms, all lined with Renaissance masterpieces. I knew a little about art from my general education classes as an undergraduate, but the sheer volume of work in the museum was overwhelming.

Finally, Cesare pulled me to a stop in front of a painting so realistic-looking it could have been a photograph.

Clearly from the Renaissance era, the image depicted two women. The woman in the background was dressed in rich Renaissance robes with a sword braced on her shoulder. In the foreground, a second, more humbly attired woman stood in front of the first, a basket holding the severed head of a man perched on her hip. Both women were looking to the right of the painting, as if they had just heard a noise.

I leaned in and read the title: *Judith and her Maidservant, 1613.*

Ah.

Naturally, I knew the apocryphal Biblical story of my namesake. Judith was a Jewish widow who, along with her maid, infiltrated the enemy Assyrian encampment in an effort to save her doomed countrymen. Judith ingratiated herself with the Assyrian general, Holofernes. One night, as Holofernes lay in a drunken stupor, Judith decapitated him and carried his head away in a basket as proof of his demise. The Assyrians were so demoralized by the loss of their leader, they retreated and Israel was saved.

The story, though widely considered fictional, was one of female empowerment and resourcefulness.

I've always liked being named Judith.

The painting showed Judith after beheading Holofernes, strong and in charge, determined to seize the day and save her people.

"You like this painting." Cesare leaned toward me.

I nodded.

He smiled. "Let me make it better for you."

He pointed to the artist's name under the title: Artemisia Gentileschi.

He acted like that was important somehow. But, not being an art history major myself, the name meant nothing. I had never heard of this person. It merely looked like an Italian mouthful.

I raised my eyebrows and shot a glance at Cesare. "Why is he important?"

"The painter? Artemisia?" Cesare suddenly chuckled. "*She* is widely considered one of the most progressive and talented painters of the early seventeenth century."

She?!

Shock jolted me, followed immediately by a wash of shame. How could I have assumed that the name was male? In looking at it now, it obviously could be a woman's name: Artemisia.

Man, was I sexist or what? My feminist self shook her head in dismay.

My emotions must have sprawled across my face because Cesare continued to smile.

"It's an honest mistake," he said. "For the record, Gentileschi is one of only a handful of female painters in this museum, so statistically, you were correct to assume the painter would be male. Logic is simply failing you in this."

I rolled my eyes at the dig.

Cesare laughed again, low and delighted.

"Gentileschi was prolific," he continued. "And nearly all of her paintings feature women in positions of power or strength. She rarely painted men by themselves."

I moved closer to the painting, studying the fine detail of Judith's dress, the careful drape of the maidservant's sleeve. I liked that both Judith and the maid felt like real people. Neither of them were too pretty or steeped in idealized concepts of feminine beauty.

"Fascinating," I said.

I suddenly wanted to know everything about Artemisia Gentileschi.

How had she survived as a painter in a man's world? How had she received her training? Why had I never heard of her, when she was clearly so talented?

"Are there more of her works?" I asked.

"Follow me." Cesare continued to smile, a secret sorta thing.

What was up his sleeve? More rope?

Note to self—never think you have the upper hand with Cesare D'Angelo.

But I followed him.

He led the way through the throngs of people, eventually reaching behind to snag my hand again.

His palm was dry and broad, his fingers easily folding around mine. Charged energy surged along the connection.

My heart hammered in my chest and a giddy smile seemed to have taken up permanent residence on my face.

I barely recognized myself. Who was this woman with the whopping crush on a virtual stranger?

And why couldn't I get her to care about how illogical it all was?

I had never felt like this before. Not with Steve. Not with anyone.

Cesare pulled me along corridors and through crowded rooms, sneaking glances at me over his shoulder, until we reached another back room.

He stopped before another large painting.

I glanced at the plaque: Artemisia Gentileschi, *Judith Slaying Holofernes, 1614-1620.*

This rendition of Judith and Holofernes was more graphic. Whereas the previous painting showed the aftermath of Judith and her maidservant stealing away with Holofernes' head in a basket, this version showed Judith in the very act of beheading the Assyrian general, blade biting into his bloody throat.

The image was brutally violent. A strong light source cut through the painting in a column of illumination, leaving items either bright or dark with little in between. *Chiaroscuro*, the painting technique was called—literally translated as *lightdark*. Seething limbs and blood and swirling fabric trapped my eye, keeping me glued to the figures.

There was a tangible physicality to the painting. Judith sawing at Holoferne's neck with one hand, the other hand firmly wrapped around his hair, pulling his head back to expose his throat. The crosspiece of Judith's sword pressing deep into Holofernes forearm as he tried to fight her off.

The painting was . . . angry. Furious. Raging. Wrathful. I could *feel* Judith's desperation to behead this man, to stop him from hurting her people.

Unbidden, my heartbeat sped up, and I found myself leaning closer and closer to it, wanting to absorb every nuance. How had Artemisia so carefully captured all this detail? How did she *make* me feel these things? Her brushwork was so small and fine, the paint was practically part of the canvas.

"*Attenzione!*" A guard barked.

Cesare pulled me back. "Not too close," he murmured.

I nodded and darted a glance at the guard, who was now watching me with a close eye.

"She looks the same," I said, moving closer to Cesare, my shoulder mere millimeters from his chest. The heat of him radiated around me.

The more I studied it, the more the figure of Judith looked similar to the previous version. Holofernes certainly looked the same with his wide face and shaggy beard.

"Yes, all of Gentileschi's versions of Judith and Holofernes bear a resemblance to each other."

"Amazing. I love her sense of consistency. Like she wanted to tell the story in brief moments, so she kept the characters, so to speak, looking the same."

"It's more than that."

I turned to Cesare, a question mark in my eyes. "What do you mean?"

"You wondered earlier why you had never heard of Artemisia Gentileschi. The reason is a typical tale of misogyny and patriarchal hierarchy."

Oh. I liked those scholarly buzzwords on Cesare's oh-so-fine lips: *misogyny, patriarchal hierarchy.*

More of his catnip for the educated woman.

"Men have never taken kindly to being upstaged by a talented woman." I flicked a hand toward the painting.

"That, too."

I angled my head. "What happened?"

Cesare folded his arms across his chest. "Gentileschi was sexually assaulted—"

"What? She was raped? Artemisia?"

"Yes."

I couldn't repress my shudder of horror.

Cesare's eyebrows raised, agreeing with me. "Gentileschi was assaulted and raped by her mentor and teacher, a man named Tassi. Gentileschi's father took the man to court over the incident, pressing charges. It was a huge, public scandal, as Gentileschi's family had enough influence to make it an issue. She is one of the few women from history to challenge her rapist in court."

"Good for her."

"Yes. But she paid a steep price for her actions. Later historians, particularly Victorians, haven't looked kindly on her."

I snorted. "Typical. The patriarchy doesn't like a woman who refuses to stay silent."

"True. Even at the time, people were scandalized that Gentileschi would opt for a public trial rather than go into disgraced hiding."

"Hide and be ashamed because of a man's actions toward her?"

"Precisely. But Gentileschi fought him instead, refusing to be cowed into silence. She won, by the way."

Admiration blazed through me, respect for a woman who refused to go quietly to her fate.

Cesare continued, pointing at the painting, "Throughout her career, Gentileschi painted the subject of Judith and Holofernes over and over. And in every single one, Gentileschi paints herself as Judith and her rapist as Holofernes."

Oh!

I looked back at the painting, abruptly seeing it as Artemisia cutting off the head of her rapist, taking back her power.

Emotion choked me.

I didn't know why, precisely.

Just . . . the thought of Artemisia, trying to succeed in a man's world and surely feeling helpless and powerless over and over, raped and abandoned, eventually using the only means at her disposal to fight back against her attacker, even if only symbolically.

Clearly stating, Y*ou may have beaten me, but you didn't defeat me. I will still roar.*

No wonder her work seethed with a palpable anger.

I found myself blinking back tears, my throat tight and aching.

"This gets to you." Cesare closed the remaining inch between us, his chest skimming my shoulder and flooding me with awareness.

I swallowed, trying to ignore the urge to sink back into him.

"Yeah—" My voice nearly broke. I took a deep breath. "There's just something about a woman fighting it out in a man's world nearly four hundred years ago. Fierce and proud, refusing to back down, because she felt her own self-worth and was determined to be valued and respected as a human being. It's humbling and inspiring."

Silence.

And then . . .

"You have no proof of that."

"What?" I turned my head to him.

"You have no proof that's what she did."

"Uh, hello? Yes, I do. Look at the painting. She clearly was taking a dig at her rapist here."

"There's no way to prove it."

"That's silly! Of course, you can. It's so obvious. You just *feel* it when you—"

I stopped. And then fully turned around to face Cesare.

He had the most manufactured innocent expression on his face, mouth quirked up at one side.

"Go on," he nudged, "you were saying something about *feeling* . . ."

I sighed.

We engaged in a staring contest for a few moments.

"Fine." I glared at him. "I get your point. I am using *feelings* to derive conclusions about something that isn't really measurable. Emotion can inform decisions. Happy?"

To Cesare's credit, he didn't gloat. Well, not too much.

His grin was definitely smug, however.

"But I would argue that in the case of Artemisia, there is enough circumstantial evidence to draw conclusions. I still have this medal—" I tapped it against my chest. "—so you have to give me some credit here."

"I would never dream of arguing with the medal." Cesare deadpanned the words, but the twinkle in his eye said differently.

"All right, Mr. Smartypants. Show me some more Artemisia paintings. You got me hooked."

"With pleasure."

Like before, Cesare wrapped his fingers around mine and pulled me along behind him.

The rest of the morning and early afternoon passed in a blur of rosy happiness.

Cesare knew the museum well, showing me painting after painting. He even slipped into the museum gift shop and bought me several postcards of Artemisia Gentileschi's work. I asked questions about his art acquisitions business. He had endless curiosity about my veterinarian degree and what I had done to earn my award medallion.

It was an idyllic few hours.

A beautiful memory in truth.

Finally, we had lingered long enough and I knew we needed to find Kimberly and Sandra.

Cesare and I were making our way back downstairs, walking down a long corridor with windows on one side and rooms branching off periodically along the other.

Abruptly, he stopped, freezing as if he had hit a hard wall, utterly immobile.

I stumbled into him, but he remained rooted, eyes firmly looking ahead, shoulders tense, lips thinned.

"Cesare?" I wrapped my hand around his, moving to his side. "You okay?"

Nothing. No reaction.

He simply stared forward, gaze unfocused.

"Cesare?" I said louder, waving a hand in front of his eyes.

Again, no reaction.

He had done this yesterday, hadn't he? When we were facing the Ponte Vecchio?

My heart sped up.

What was wrong? Was this some sort of fit? Was he having an absence seizure? I had read about them during one of my general medical classes.

Would he collapse next? At what point should I get help?

I took a step away from him, intent on asking one of the security guards for help, when Cesare sagged.

He came back to life, like his mind had been highjacked and taken elsewhere and then suddenly re-injected into him. Just as suddenly as it had started, Cesare was back. He raised a hand to his forehead.

I clutched his hand in mine. "What happened? You okay? You had me on the verge of a freak-out there."

"Yeah," he nodded.

"You sure?" I asked. "It looked like you had a seizure of some sort. Maybe we should get help."

"No. Don't need help." He shook his head. "I'm good. Give me a second."

He continued to massage his temples with the fingers of his loose hand.

He looked fine. His color hadn't changed and his breathing was steady.

But something was up with him. I could *feel* it.

I moved into him, clutching his hand in both of mine.

"You sure you're okay?" I had to ask again.

"Yes," he nodded. "There's nothing to be done about it. The fits . . . pass. When I'm with you, it's all okay."

I should have asked: *What about when you're not with me? Are things not okay? And what does that even mean?*

Hindsight is always twenty/twenty.

"Well if you're sure," I said instead.

Abruptly, I realized Cesare was really close to me. Like . . . if I leaned my lips two inches forward and up, our mouths would meet.

I should have instantly turned away. I didn't.

His pupils dilated and his eyes dipped to my mouth. We still held hands, fingers intertwined between us.

"Judith," he whispered, his tone almost pained. Like I brought him incredible joy and yet terrified him at the same time.

Or perhaps I was simply projecting.

Damn *feeling* again.

He brought his free hand to my chin, tracing my jaw with his thumb, instantly flooding my endocrine system with boozy endorphins.

A part of my brain told me to stand back; that I was getting in too deep, too quickly with this man. That I was behaving illogically.

But I couldn't seem to care.

He was tender and kind and funny and sexy and made me want to be my fullest self.

The thought was as terrifying as it was thrilling.

But you're leaving tomorrow, so the point is moot, remember?

And I was still technically in a relationship with Steve. So there was that.

I pulled back. Not because I was afraid or worried or didn't want to be so close to Cesare.

No.

It was precisely the opposite. He made me feel and want with a vicious ache, and I wasn't sure how to channel all those unexpected emotions into something that wasn't borderline neurotic.

For his part, Cesare watched me, that same open wonder and pain on his face.

"You leave tomorrow?" His offhand words jarred me.

Was he reading my mind now?

"Uhm . . . I, well . . . yes," I stammered out, tucking hair behind my ear. "I mean, that's the plan."

A beat.

Ask me, I silently pleaded. *Ask me if I have to go.*

He took a deep breath. "Do you have to leave? Could you stay?"

His questions were *hosanna* and *holy crap* and *howdidheknowtoaskmethat?!*

My brain reeled. Could he read minds, too?

Of course, my stupid, drunken hormones instantly threw a party at the thought of spending more time with him. They were such saboteurs.

What to say?

"I . . . I suppose we could," I stammered. "We're off to Venice, but we don't have any reservations or anything. We were just going to show up at the youth hostel. We could stay for another day, if Kimberly and Sandra are okay with it."

If I stayed one more day, it would be that much harder to leave him. I knew this, and yet my greedy heart wasn't ready to go.

One more day. Just one more.

"A day," he murmured, eyes flitting down to my mouth. "Is that all you can spare?"

Could I stay longer? We had no real set agenda, just a general schedule that could be flexible.

"There is an apartment above my mother's," he continued. "It sits empty. You and your friends could stay there as long as you wished. My mother would look out for you. She has an enormous heart. And . . . we could continue to see each other."

Silence.

My mind raced, trying to think of strong reasons why I should say no.

I barely knew this guy. Something was up with his health. He magically knew when to pluck small children from large rivers. I had steady, dependable Steve waiting at home.

"I can't believe I'm even contemplating this," I whispered.

But I could only find motives to stay.

I liked Cesare. I wanted to know him better. I would have deep regrets if I left tomorrow.

It didn't escape me that all my reasons were based on emotions, not logic.

He tightened his grip on my hand.

"Stay." One word. It was all he offered.

I felt it keenly then.

I teetered on the precipice.

Cesare D'Angelo was entirely unknown.

He sensed my hesitation.

"You should probably leave," he murmured. "It would be best for you. I'm not sure I won't cause you heartache in the end."

I stilled.

Oooookay.

Unexpected, that.

"You'll cause me heartache?" I repeated, wanting to be sure I had heard him right.

"Yes."

"How so?"

"I yearn to *keep* you. *That* is the heartache."

I melted. Italian men and their one-liners.

"Think about it," he whispered into my ear. "Think about staying longer, *mon angelo*. Stay much longer."

I can't believe we're actually doing this." I set my backpack on the couch. "I think it's a brilliant idea," Kimberly chirped as she moved through the open doorway to join me. "I'm all about a free place to stay."

"This is going to save us so much money. Do you think Cesare meant it when he said we could stay as long as we want?" Sandra asked coming in behind her.

"Yeah," I replied. "I really think he does."

"Huh," was Sandra's reply. "This is going to be perfect."

Kimberly nodded. "We have our Eurail passes, so we can hop a train whenever we want. We'll just take day trips from Florence."

Obviously, I hadn't been able to say goodbye to Cesare.

After the Uffizi the day before, we had met back up with Sandra and Kimberly. Then, Cesare had insisted on treating us to a lengthy lunch/ dinner.

We had laughed and talked, arguing and discussing everything from the fallout of Ronald Reagan being shot to favorite punk rock bands (Me? The Police. Cesare? The Clash).

Throughout dinner, thoughts of Artemisia Gentileschi had lingered, the courage it had to have taken for her to stand up to her rapist. I recognized that I was using intuition (i.e. emotion) to infer Artemisia's motivations. Which meant that my logical brain had to admit . . . Cesare maybe had a teeny-tiny point with the whole feelings-can-be-used-as-valid-scientific-data thing.

Curse him.

Afterward, Cesare took us on a walking tour of the city, pointing out favorite sites and telling stories. He had another small episode as we strolled down a side street, pausing as if looking up at wisteria winding its way up a medieval building, his hesitation so brief, only I noticed it.

All in all, the day was nearly fairytale perfect.

It was not lost on me that I hadn't spared a second thought for Steve the whole evening.

But maybe that was how things worked when it came to basic human biology. Whatever was newest and most exciting was what drew our attention.

That said, it felt like there was so much unexplored between Cesare and me. I wanted to know more about him. What caused his seizures? How had he known to save the little boy in the river?

The logical part of my brain found my intense connection with him fascinating. How could biology work like that? I certainly wasn't in love with him, and I wasn't sure love even existed. But if anyone could convince me of its reality, it would be Cesare D'Angelo.

The scientist in me wasn't ready to give up on this experiment yet.

Thankfully, Kimberly and Sandra were supportive of the idea. They liked saving some money and I liked having them around. I certainly wasn't naive enough to stay in one of Cesare's apartments without some backup.

It turned out that Cesare owned the *entire* apartment building—palazzo, as he called it. The ground floor was a set of offices for his business.

The next floor was his apartment. The third floor was his mother's apartment.

We got the top floor—an empty apartment Cesare said they used for out-of-town guests and relatives.

"This place is nice." Kimberly pointed to the beamed ceiling. "There's a narrow kitchen through the wall here and some bedrooms down the hallway."

Sandra wandered over to the window, pushing aside the curtains. "And the view out of this window is gorgeous. Just rooftops and Florence."

"These Italian apartments are weird," Kimberly said. "Why have a bunch of rooms branching off a central hallway? If this were my apartment, I would knock down the walls between this room and the kitchen and make one huge great room. Imagine how amazing these beams would look in a larger space."

I twirled around the room. She did have a valid point. It would be stunning if it were all opened up. Maybe someday a future owner would to that.

"Well, ladies." Sandra clapped her hands together. "Let's play rock, paper, scissors to see who gets what bedroom?"

THE NEXT SEVERAL DAYS PASSED IN a haze of fun.

Cesare showed us around the city. We climbed to the top of the Duomo and got an after-hours tour of the Accademia Museum with its statue of Michelangelo's *David*.

We shopped in the markets of San Lorenzo and drank *caffè* and ate *panini* from street cafes. Kimberly, Sandra and I took day trips out from Florence on the days that Cesare worked, visiting Siena and Arezzo.

Cesare continued to have those odd seizures. They were frequent enough for me to worry. What was going on? Was he epileptic in some way, having absence seizures? Were they sometimes worse, moving into grand mal seizures?

Whenever I would ask about it, he would change the topic and generally act like it was no big deal. Part of me wanted to believe him, but another part of me—yes, the part that was irrational and emotional—felt like those episodes were important somehow.

The more time I spent with him, the more invested I felt. Cesare D'Angelo was attractive deliciousness dipped in enigma sauce, and he had both my emotions and logic hungry for more, more, more.

An eagerness clung to him. Like he was determined to drink life down to the dregs, seeking the most out of everything. No caution. No hesitation. No fear.

The biggest problem? Or was it the solution?

Being with Cesare was so . . . easy. Not uncomplicated. Not simple. But easy in the sense that I felt my most true, most authentic self around him. I didn't have to hide or pretend or tiptoe.

Cesare accepted me just as I was and wanted nothing more than for me to just, well, be *me*.

I wasn't sure how or if I was going to deal with all these unexpected emotions.

So I didn't.

Cesare helped me get a *carte telefonica*—a telephone calling card—and showed me how to dial the States so I could keep my family up-to-date about my whereabouts.

At first, he had insisted I just use his phone, but I couldn't ask him to pay the high charges. I had heard him on the phone with international clients in his office and the phone counter whizzed on those calls, clicking rapidly. As Cesare explained it, each *scatto* or click of the little counter by the corded phone cost a certain amount. The man was already housing us. No need to rack up huge phone bills for him, too.

But it was nice to chat with my mom and my sister. I even gave into my guilt-over-not-feeling-guilt when it came to Steve and called him.

Steve was . . . Steve.

He talked about his plans for residency come September and the biking trip he was taking with his brother. I talked about the museums I had visited and the things I'd seen.

He mentioned he'd gone clubbing with a group of friends and said they'd missed me.

I didn't say anything about Cesare. (Was that bad of me? I wasn't sure. Again guilt-over-not-feeling-guilt there.)

We both confirmed that we were on a break and I'd call him again in a couple weeks.

So, ya know, romantic times.

It was a contrast to the heady excitement I felt around Cesare. I kept expecting it to fade, but if anything, it increased.

I liked that Cesare never hovered or seemed possessive. He was simply attentive and kind and endlessly patient.

A solid ninety-three percent of me appreciated that space. That he was respectful of me.

But that other seven percent was flabbergasted that he hadn't attempted to kiss me. Clearly, kissing tourists was a thing. Kimberly's constantly rising tally of smooches proved this. (Two weeks in and she was already at nine kisses . . . again, I didn't know whether I should be impressed or appalled.)

And yet with me and Cesare?

Nothing.

He clearly liked me and, given how often he found an excuse to touch me, he seemed to *need* physical contact. As if he were constantly reassuring himself that I really was here. As for me, I flirted and took every shameless excuse to touch him in return, casual brushes of his arm, gratuitous pats on the back.

Basically, it was obvious that I wanted him to kiss me.

Correction.

I really wanted Cesare D'Angelo to kiss me.

Like . . . really, really wanted him to kiss me.

And he still hadn't kissed me. Yes, we held hands and air-kissed in greeting, and he had kissed my forehead three times, but that was it.

Sandra and Kimberly kept telling me to kiss him first. That Cesare was probably being a gentleman and waiting for me to take the lead.

I realized, awkward as it was, I might have to take matters into my own hands . . . ehr, lips.

A WEEK AFTER ARRIVING IN FLORENCE, I tripped down the stairs of the D'Angelo's palazzo and let myself out of the main door. Mist rose from the wet pavement in the early morning light, glistening in the already bright sun. Sandra and Kimberly weren't with me as they were headed to Pisa for the day.

Outside the door, Cesare waited in the arched passageway that ran between the street and the courtyard area behind his palazzo. His eyes lit up upon seeing me.

Today was for Cesare and me. One more beautiful memory.

Cesare had asked me to meet him early this morning to tour the Museo San Marco. I had no idea what it was or what it housed, but if Cesare said it would be worthwhile, I trusted him.

He smiled as I stopped in front of him. He was wearing a smart looking suit and tie today, *molto italiano,* with his hair slicked back and mirror shades over his eyes, a cup of coffee held in his hand. But interestingly, he had a Polaroid camera around his neck in a leather case, a bit of unexpected tourist kitsch.

He had asked me to wear a skirt, so I was dressed in a flirty, summer sundress which Kimberly had called 'smokin' hot' as I walked out the door.

I could feel his eyes drifting over me, lingering in the way that spoke louder than words that he liked what he saw.

So why don't you want to kiss me? Be the Italian man.

"*Ciao, bella.*" He reached for me, pulling me into a lingering Italian air-kiss greeting, breathing deeply.

I sank into the casual embrace.

"For you, *tesora mia.*" He handed over the styrofoam cup of coffee.

A thrill of surprise warmed me. "Thank you. How thoughtful."

Truly, it was. I couldn't think that Steve had ever done something thoughtful like this. Too practical, I supposed.

That said, Steve also knew I was super picky about how I liked my coffee, so he preferred to avoid the potential land mine catastrophe of ordering it for me.

Cesare eyed me, obviously waiting for me to take a sip.

I was nervous I wouldn't be able to control a grimace if I didn't like it. I didn't want him thinking his sweet gesture was unappreciated.

"You a photographer, too?" I used the question as an excuse to distract his gaze, touching the strap of the camera with my free hand.

He glanced down.

I took a sip of the coffee.

Flavor and cream and sugar all perfectly blended with ice hit my taste buds in a knockout punch. Perfection.

Wow.

My eyes rolled back into my head and I may have moaned.

I eagerly took another long drink.

Cesare laughed.

"How did you know how I like my coffee?" I had to ask.

He still grinned but something hesitant filled his expression, as if my question were hard to answer.

"I have my ways," was all he said.

"More of your . . . *feelings?*" I liked the teasing, flirty tone of my voice.

"Something like that," he murmured in reply, a grin tugging at his mouth.

I rolled my eyes. "Or maybe you just asked Sandra?"

"That, too."

I took another healthy sip, much-needed caffeine flooding my system and perking me fully awake.

"So . . . are you a photographer?" I repeated the question.

"Not particularly." That fleeting melancholy washed his expression. "But I wanted to make sure I had something to remember you by, Judith Campbell."

His words jump-started an ache somewhere behind my heart.

Was he already thinking about when I left? Anticipating it?

I mean, of course I was going to leave. Duh. It wasn't like I could stay.

"A beautiful memory?"

A sad smile. "Precisely, for both of us."

No! I want more than just a single warm, fuzzy memory. I want lots and lots of memories. My stupid heart practically shrieked the words, rattling its cage. *How's about we start with a kiss?*

Of course, that thought had nutjob written all over it and seeing how nutjob was kinda the opposite of my logical self, I pushed it aside.

So instead of saying something about me leaving, I replied, "Well, let's take a photo then." I set my coffee down on a stone ledge under the archway.

He unsnapped the camera cover and, with one hand, turned it around to face us, gently pulling me into his chest with the other.

I repeat.

He pulled me into his chest.

A few things about that.

First, wow.

Second, double wow.

Third, why did he smell so freaking good?

Fourth, could we kiss now?

All of which meant I took shameless advantage of the situation and snuggled in tighter to him. I could feel the flex of his chest muscles underneath my hand, the firmness of his pectorals, the latent strength in his upper body.

More significantly, he relaxed the second I melted into him, like everything suddenly went right in his world. His lungs deflated and his hand tightened around my waist, his head automatically canting to rest against mine.

My eyes fluttered shut for a second. Did he *have* to feel so right?

And again . . . given that he clearly liked me and I obviously liked him—

Why no kissy?

Don't get me wrong. The hug was glorious. I wouldn't have minded *more* hugging, but my question still remained.

Cesare took two photos of us snuggled together, one after the other. Me tucked into him, forehead against his cheek, arms and palms pressed against his chest, smiling at the camera. Him with a hand splayed across the small of my back, face grinning at the camera, eyes hidden behind his sunglasses, the mirror surface reflecting the bulky Polaroid.

With a final squeeze, he let me go and handed one of the photos to me, waving the other in the air.

"One for each of us," he explained.

A souvenir of our beautiful memory.

Oddly, I suddenly found my throat tight. I turned my head, blinking my stinging eyes as I took another sip of my iced coffee and let Cesare help me into the taxi that had just pulled up.

Was Cesare content to have me as a beautiful memory, then? Was that why he wasn't kissing me? Or was he conflicted like myself?

So far, he had seemed happy to be with me, maybe even a little desperate. Like I was a luxury treat he was allowing himself—a binge before going on a diet.

Which made no sense logically. Why did I intuitively think that?

Emotion was clearly in the driver seat of my life currently, having stuffed Logic in the trunk. I still hadn't decided if that was a good or bad thing. Emotion was certainly a more exciting driver than Logic, if I chose to anthropomorphize them. Which, it seemed, I was.

I finished the coffee in giant gulps, as if it would give me clarity.

It didn't.

Though at least my confusion was now also nicely caffeinated.

And I was even more determined to claim that kiss. If Cesare was to be only a fun story I swapped with other ladies in the old folks' home fifty years from now, I wanted it to be as spectacular as possible.

Operation Kiss Cesare was so happening.

6

Twenty minutes later, the taxi dropped us off at the edge of a large city square. Trees and a small park sat in the middle of the piazza with a large, Baroque-looking church running along one side.

Cesare threaded his hand through mine and tugged me across the piazza to the church, camera hitting his chest as we walked.

We were up early, before the museums had fully opened, so the streets were generally empty of tourists. With humidity rising off the pavement in the morning air, Florence had a magical quality.

"Tell me about this Museo San Marco." I tossed my empty coffee cup into a nearby trash can. "You've been secretive about it."

He smiled, a mixture of mystery and teasing humor.

"You will love this place, *cara*," was all he gave me as we crossed to the front of the large church facade.

Like he had at the Uffizi, Cesare knocked on an age-darkened wood door tucked into a recess of the facade. He removed his sunglasses and gave my hand a squeeze as we waited.

An elderly man in monk's robes opened the door and, no lie, *bowed* to us, motioning for us to cross into the dark room beyond.

For his part, Cesare changed somewhat, too. Gone was the unpretentious, amiable person I had been getting to know.

Instead, Cesare straightened his spine and talked to the monk with a calm, if somewhat formal, reserve. He and the man spoke for a few moments, the man continuing to bob his head occasionally. I heard the monk say the word *signore*—sir or mister—several times.

I clung to Cesare's hand, unsure what was going on.

After a few minutes, the monk turned around to speak to another brother who had walked into the room.

"What's with the bowing?" I whispered. "Do monks always bow?"

He gave me a side-eyed look. "No."

I raised my eyebrows. *Continue.*

Cesare smiled but said nothing.

"Tell me," I needled him.

"What? And ruin the surprise?"

"What surprise?" My eyes narrowed.

The monk turned back to us, speaking again in Italian, though this time I clearly heard him say, *mio signore.*

Mio signore?

People had been calling Cesare *signore* all week. But what was *mio*? Was it like *mi* in Spanish? Did it mean *my*?

The monk said it again—*mio signore.*

So *mio signore* meant 'my mister'? Why would Cesare be 'my' anything?

But given that the monk punctuated his *mio signore* with another bow, a different thought hit me.

Logic did, after all, have its uses.

I grabbed Cesare's elbow before he could follow the monk out of the room.

"Wait a second—did he just call you, 'my lord'?"

Cesare looked back at me, gaze surprised. "Your Italian is better than I thought."

And then Cesare followed the monk.

Out.

The.

Door.

Like he hadn't just dropped a huge bomb on me.

I barely managed to not screech 'You're a freaking Italian LORD?!' at his back like a banshee.

Instead, I hissed the words in his ear once I caught up with him.

"You're a freaking Italian LORD?!"

Cesare ignored me for a moment—though he clearly heard my words because his lips twitched—and instead smiled politely at the monk. The brother opened another doorway into an arched cloister and motioned us through.

The door closed, the monk remaining behind.

Cesare and I were alone.

I barely noticed the cloister with its charming arches and beautifully landscaped grassy area. I folded my arms and lasered in on Cesare.

His face was open but wary.

It was also a sign of his intelligence that he didn't make me repeat my question.

"Yes," he said, "I am an Italian lord. Well, a *conte* to be exact."

"*Conte?*" Okay. Wow. "What's that?"

"In English? A count or an earl, I suppose."

My poor stunned brain struggled to catch up. Which explained why my next sentence came out more than a little accusatory:

"And at what point were you going to tell me that you were an *earl?* I've known you for almost a week!"

"Well, one hardly leads with, 'Hello, Beautiful, I'm an earl.'"

"Really? Because I'm pretty sure most earls do. It's kinda the point of being an earl, isn't it?"

"No. Really it's not."

Sheesh. No wonder he hadn't kissed me. Those were practically royal lips I had been lusting.

"Then what does being an earl mean?" I asked.

He shrugged. It was a decidedly Italian movement, not so much dismissive as nonchalant. "Very little. It means that with a phone call or two, I can arrange an early visit to the monastery of San Marco." He waved a hand in a circle, indicating the building around us. "I also have a very fancy seal I can use when I sign a letter with my title."

"A fancy seal?"

"Yes. Extremely fancy. Earl fancy." He deadpanned. "Coat of arms and everything. I hold up a lofty pinky finger when I use it."

"Funny." My lips twitched. "So . . . you have a specific title?"

"Yes."

Silence.

I tilted my head, as if to say, *really?* Then I rolled my index finger. *Tell me then.*

Cesare took the hint. "I'm known as *il Conte del Maledetto.*"

"The Earl of Maledetto?" I translated. "Where is Maledetto?"

"Maledetto isn't precisely a place." A pause. "It's more like a state of being."

Okay. "What does *maledetto* mean then?"

Cesare pinched the bridge of his nose, as if the answer were difficult somehow. But he did reply:

"*Maledetto* means damned."

I blinked, visibly flinching.

"Wait?" My brain put it all together. "Your title is *The Damned Earl?*"

He nodded, fingertips pressed into his forehead.

I wasn't sure what I had expected his answer to be, but it hadn't been *that.*

The *Damned* Earl.

"Why *that* title? You're Mr. Italian Aristocracy living the dream in downtown Florence. That's sorta the opposite of damnation."

"The title is not anything I chose."

"But an ancestor chose it, right?"

"In a way."

"In a way? What on earth did your ancestors do to end up with such a name? It doesn't seem like the kind of label people would be lining up for."

Cesare chuckled, the sound decidedly unamused. "No. They most certainly did not."

More silence.

"You're not going to clue me in to the accursed thing they did?"

He shrugged again, letting his eyes drift over the courtyard, the stone, anywhere but me.

That same sadness flitted across his face. "Damnation comes in different forms."

"That's kinda deep, your damned lordship."

His mouth turned up at the edges. "Is it gonna be like that now?"

I tapped my lips. "Yeah, pretty sure I have a least a solid four dozen damnation jokes in me. Can't be letting all that lordliness go to your head."

Cesare chuckled, shoving his hands into his pockets, head leaning back, looking up to the sky. His chuckle was part humor, part pain and part marveling. Like he was flabbergasted and wondrous he was here with me.

He did not, however, answer my question.

"Cesare? You gonna spill the damned beans?"

Another reluctant chuckle before he finally turned back to me. "Come, *bella*." He extended a hand toward me.

"You're not going to tell me?" I didn't take his hand.

That sadness returned. "No, today is too beautiful and bright to bring such darkness into it."

What did that mean? And being deliberately vague and mysterious wasn't doing anything to quell my curiosity.

I mentally let it go.

Besides, I had Operation Kiss Cesare to worry about. Did earls kiss commoners like myself? Or maybe damned ones made an exception?

Cesare studied my face before moving his fingers, encouraging me on. "Let me show you the monastery of San Marco."

I tucked my hand into his.

"Yeah, why are we here, anyway? Trying to salvage your damned soul?" I asked.

"Something like that. Or maybe I just want to impress the Girl with the Gold Award." He waggled his eyebrows.

I blushed. "I can't believe I've been waving my stupid award around in front of a real-live *earl.*"

"Well, I became an earl by being born." He rested his palm on his chest. "It was a very difficult task and involved at least nine months of solid work on my mother's part. You, on the other hand, simply studied and worked hard for years."

I laughed despite myself.

"Well, Mr. Damned Earl, tell me what's so special about this monastery."

"I am glad you asked, Golden Girl—"

"Gold *Award* Girl," I corrected him.

"No, I like Golden Girl." He reached out and lifted a sun-bleached strand of my hair into the sun. It gleamed golden-bright.

"Alright, your lordship." I smiled at him, squeezing his hand. "The monastery. Why did you bring me here?"

"The short answer? It's one of my favorite places in all of Florence. Lots of *feeling.*" He wiggled his eyebrows again.

I laughed.

He pulled on my hand and we walked down the archway.

"So . . . San Marco," I prompted.

"Yes. There are lots of reasons why I love this place, but specifically, San Marco was home to Fra Angelico—"

"That name sounds familiar."

We crossed the cloister and passed into the refectory.

"It should. Fra Angelico was an innovative painter and artist during the early Renaissance. But he was also a devoted monk and follower of Christ. He lived here in San Marco and spent his time decorating the spartan cells of his fellow monks with frescoes of scenes from the Bible. The older part of the monastery has been turned into a museum, so we can walk through the cells and hallways that he decorated."

"Wow. Impressive."

"It is."

Cesare led me through the refectory and into the enormous church proper, explaining as we went, pointing to luminous frescoes on the walls.

The monastery wasn't covered in paintings like some churches I had seen. Instead, frescoes were placed discreetly here and there, like little hidden gems.

While we walked, he had another of his odd episodes. He paused and stared ahead for no reason I could discern. It didn't last long, maybe only thirty seconds, but it was . . . concerning. Another absence seizure of some kind.

Cesare said the seizures were nothing and clearly expected me to just roll with them. So, I did. I couldn't figure him out. He was so open about some things and then a bank vault about others.

We climbed up the stairs to the monks' dormitory, Cesare motioning me ahead of him. I wondered why for about two seconds, continuing to climb upward, and then my eyes landed on the breathtaking fresco at the top of the stairs. I recognized the familiar scene instantly:

Mary and the angel Gabriel.

The painting was set in an arched courtyard, not unlike the cloister we had just left. It depicted the Annunciation—Gabriel appearing to the Virgin Mary to tell her she would bear the Christ child. The image was exquisitely drawn but sparse in its details: Mary's humble clothing, the bare stucco of the cloister arches, the draped folds of Gabriel's robes.

I stood transfixed for a solid minute, unable to take my eyes away. Why did the painting feel so perfect here? A surprise and yet a completion? Worshipful austere reverence.

The *sha-shunk whirrrr* of Cesare's Polaroid sounded behind me.

I spun around to see him walking up the stairs toward me, shaking another photo.

He ignored my questioning look and instead motioned to my right, pointing down a long hallway. Rounded arched doorways punctuated the corridor at regular intervals, wooden roof beams soaring overhead.

"These are the monks' cells." He pointed to the first room on the right. "This bedroom here is my favorite."

I walked into the tiny room, so small it barely fit a sparse bed. But the white-washed walls extended upward to the roof beams, giving the illusion of sailing toward heaven. Nestled between the arched window and the doorway was another fresco—a smaller version of the Annunciation out in the hall.

As with the other painting, I stared up at it, taking in the serenity of the scene—Mary humbly kneeling, the angel rimmed in gold.

I could see why Cesare liked this room. The barren intimacy of the space made the beauty of the painting stand out more starkly.

"I see you like this," he murmured softly behind me.

I turned to him, brows drawn down.

He was close behind me—where else could he go in this minuscule space?—so close that I could see the mossy flecks in his hazel eyes. The crazy magnetic attraction between us swirled in the tiny room, pinging off the walls and amplifying.

I was finding it hard to breathe.

"See me like what?" I asked.

"Like the angel. Golden and luminous. My Golden Girl."

Back to that, was he?

"I'm hardly an angel, Cesare."

"Oh, *bella*, but you are." He placed a scalding hand on my waist and shifted me into the pool of light spilling through the window. "Turn toward the window."

I shot him a scrunched-mouth look, but then did as he asked. He moved in front of me, pulling his camera free.

He snapped a Polaroid, shaking it as he moved back to my side, wrapping his free arm around my waist again, mostly because the room was so small, it was nearly impossible not to.

But still, his touch jolted through me. I wanted to melt into his chest as I had an hour earlier, lose myself in the sheer joy of being with him. Breathing the same air beside Cesare for only one minute was better than spending hours with anyone else.

Dimly, my logical mind pointed out that this was a completely irrational thought. It made no sense and was completely contrary to how I had felt with previous boyfriends, Steve included.

"See," Cesare said after a moment, holding the Polaroid up. "My angel."

I stared at the image. I stood in a shaft of sunlight in my loose summer dress, the warm sun turning my hair into molten fire. The light washed my face and chest, casting me into light and dark, like Artemisia's paintings.

Even my most logical neurons had to acknowledge that I did look vaguely celestial.

"My saving angel," Cesare continued.

"Because you're the Damned Earl?" I said the words teasingly, but I wasn't so sure Cesare read them that way.

"Exactly."

Instead of leaning away, I inched forward, seeking more of him. Cesare obliged and tightened his arm around me, reeling me flush against him.

My heart hammered in my throat. I had a feeling once I started to demand pieces of him, I would never be able to get enough. I would want more and more of Cesare D'Angelo until I didn't know where I ended and he began.

And still I didn't stop. My hands pressed against his chest, fingers flexing, aching to haul him those final few inches closer and claim his mouth as my own.

"You're not damned, Cesare," I whispered in the tense silence.

"You can't know that."

"The man I saw dangling from a rope to pull a small child from the River Arno is hardly damned."

"Maybe that was penance."

"Penance? For what?"

He shrugged. "Being born, I suppose."

I snorted. "Being born is hardly a sin."

"Not true. Sometimes, it is."

"I don't believe you're damned. Have you committed murder? Hurt innocent people? Sinned greatly against your fellow man?"

"No."

"You're not damned, then. I don't know that I believe in damnation. I most certainly don't believe in it for you." My itchy fingers pressed against his chest, wanting nothing more than to fist a handful of his shirt.

"Sometimes we suffer for the sins of our fathers."

Ah. "Back to being born as a sin, are you? So it was your father who was damned?"

"Among other D'Angelos. We are prisoners, us D'Angelo men, serving time in chains of our ancestors' making."

It was an odd statement. I pulled back, expecting to see a teasing light in his eyes, but there was none.

Instead, that same age-old sadness clung to him; he looked so tired, so weary.

He swallowed and lifted a hand, brushing a lock of hair behind my ear.

That energy swirled between us.

His eyes met mine, pupils dilated, expression hooded. His gaze flicked to my mouth.

I could almost taste him, he was so close.

A kiss to seal my beautiful memory.

I pressed upward, seeking. I sincerely expected him to lean down those last few inches and kiss my mouth.

But . . . he didn't.

Instead, he dodged the kiss.

I repeat.

Cesare *dodged* my kiss.

He tilted his head back, out of reach of my lips. And as I stood there blinking in surprise, he gave me a half-smile and kissed my forehead. He took a step sideways and threaded his fingers through mine, intent on tugging me out of the cell.

I was left feeling bewildered, somewhat baffled and a lot frustrated, so I stood my ground, refusing to budge even as he pulled on my hand.

Why wouldn't he kiss me? Did he not like my girl cooties?

I was so hopelessly confused.

Cesare reeled back when I didn't move, turning around to face me, seeing my disgruntled emotions clearly written on my face.

"What's wrong, *cara?*" He swept his thumb across the back of my hand, sending goosebumps skittering.

I frowned. "You have to know I want to kiss you."

No sense beating around the bush. Where subtlety had failed, maybe a frontal assault would work.

Cesare's expression didn't change. "Yes, I have gathered as much." His words were measured, carefully laid. But he offered nothing more.

My stomach sank.

Wow. He really just didn't want to kiss me.

The knowledge was a lash across my psyche.

I shook my hand free of his, folding my arms across my chest.

So Cesare liked me enough to hang out with me, but not enough to do anything else.

That was okay. I was okay.

Who needed his stupid kisses anyway?

He stepped even closer, reading my stunned confusion. "Hey, hey now. None of that. Whatever you're thinking, it's not true."

I tried to shrug off the sting. "It's okay. You are under no obligation to kiss me. Especially if you don't want to—"

He let out a sound, like my statement was the most absurd thing he had ever heard. His eyes drifted down to my mouth, staring raptly.

"I can think of very little I'd like to do more than kiss you, *cara mia.*"

Oh!

His voice had a hoarse husky edge that scraped up my spine and caused all of me to feel so very . . . *aware.*

"Yes. Please, yes." I took a step toward him, closing the small space between us, arms reaching for him again.

He watched me through hooded eyes but did not reciprocate. I would have felt more disappointment, but heat flooded his eyes.

He wasn't lying. He *was* desperate to kiss me.

"Are you still dating Steve?" he asked.

"Steve?" My head jerked back. I froze. "What does Steve have to do with this?"

He rolled his hand—*just answer the question.*

"We're not dating, per se," I said. "We're on a break. Kissing you doesn't mean I'm cheating on him. Is that your concern?"

"Mmmm, but there is a promise there with Steve. There is still . . . potential and intention."

That was true.

I didn't know how to respond.

Cesare finally shifted. He clasped my hand in both of his, hazel eyes meeting mine with devastating sincerity.

"Judith, I ache to kiss you. But you must know, when I kiss a woman, I want it to mean something—"

"Of course it would mean something—"

"Let me finish." His gaze kept me pinned. "My kisses aren't something I throw about helter-skelter. I won't share your lips with another man or have them for only a season."

My chest tightened. My heart leapt into my throat, something raw awakening in my chest.

"I'm a stingy kisser. A miserly kisser," he continued. "When I finally kiss a woman, I want more than a handful. More than even a bunch or a wad."

He leaned all the way in to me, bringing me flush with him again, hand splayed across the small of my back.

"No, my Golden Girl, when I kiss a woman, I want *all* her kisses." He whispered the words against my mouth. "And I need her to want all of mine. And with you . . . I would want everything. I could spend a universe of lifetimes lost in you."

I was quite certain I had stopped breathing.

Uhmm . . . yes, please.

I'll take all your kisses.

He blinked.

I let out a slow breath.

"This attraction between us . . ." he murmured, eyes still fixed on my mouth.

"It's madness," I whispered.

My words shook him more awake. "No," he countered, leaning away enough to more fully meet my gaze. "The madness is me. *You* are love."

Silence.

Questions hammered my mind.

What did he mean by that? He was madness? How so? Manic, maybe. But hardly madness.

Was this part of his whole 'damnation' hang-up?

And for that matter, how was I *love*?

I was logic and reason and everything antithetical to love.

His eyes drifted back to my mouth.

"When you're ready to give me all your kisses, Judith, then I will be willing to give you all of mine. But until then . . ."

He smiled then, a devastatingly sad smile. A smile that said he knew I would never ask for all his kisses.

And I said nothing in return.

Because I was unsure.

Did I want his kisses? Yes.

But did I truly want *all* of them? All the kisses?

There I was unsure.

I understood that he wasn't asking for a serious long-term relationship, per se.

No, he was saying, 'I respect myself and yourself too much to kiss you when you still, technically, have a boyfriend. If and when you lose the boyfriend, get back to me.'

And I didn't have an answer to that.

I let him lead me out of the room after that. We talked and explored the site until the monastery officially opened and tourists flooded the hallways. I lingered in the gift shop, pouring over kitchy relics and beautiful postcards of the cloisters and artwork.

It was only as we were leaving that Cesare handed me another Polaroid.

I looked down at the photo.

Cesare had taken it from the bottom of a stairway. I stood dead center with my back to the camera, staring upward at the fresco of the Angel Gabriel, my body washed in a shaft of light.

C esare's words haunted me.

My Golden Girl, when I kiss a woman, I want all her kisses.

I admired how much Cesare respected both himself and me.

The more I thought about it, the more I wanted to be with the kind of man who would ask for all my kisses.

Steve had certainly never wanted all my kisses.

Of course, the problem remained.

Cesare was my European fling, my beautiful memory, and Steve was my long-term boyfriend. It wasn't like I could just swap one for the other, even if I were that kind of person.

Besides, the thought of breaking up with Steve felt . . . frightening.

Which really seemed like the wrong emotion when breaking up with someone, even if it was just pretend and in my head. Shouldn't I feel sad or relieved or free or wretched or *something* at the thought of losing Steve?

But no.

My brain had to make it all weird and, instead, choose to feel scared. Terrified.

Which was not logical any way whatsoever. So . . . illogical.

I still had no idea what, if anything, I was going to do about Cesare. I liked him, yes. But we barely knew each other, and he had secrets.

Besides, the man was a freaking earl, for cryin' out loud. A damned one, but I was pretty sure even damned earls rated pretty high. Though how his family line had become the damned earls, he refused to tell me. Clearly it was more involved than old gambling debts or a lousy cribbage score. More of his secrets.

Needless to say, after spending the day at San Marco, I had a fitful night's rest. I woke the next day shuffling through our apartment, desperately wanting clarity but willing to settle for coffee.

Fortunately, coffee was to be had.

I was staring at the metal moka pot on the stove, willing it to finish percolating my espresso, when Sandra walked into the kitchen.

"Please tell me there's enough espresso in there for two." She looked as tired as I felt.

I nodded. "How was Pisa?"

"Good. We spent a solid forty-five minutes getting the mandatory holding-up-the-leaning-tower photo, but it was fun."

We talked for a while, sipping espresso and swapping stories.

"Hey, I forgot to tell you. Thanks for telling Cesare how I like my coffee," I said. "He was sweet about it."

"Coffee?" Her forehead wrinkled.

"Yeah, he showed up with the most incredible iced espresso with lots of *cremina* yesterday morning. It was insanely good. Thanks for telling him."

A stretch of silence.

Sandra stared at me, face confused. "I didn't tell him, Jude. Honest."

It was my turn to feel confused. "Of course, you did. How else would he know?"

"I don't know, but I didn't tell him. And I'm sure Kim didn't either."

"Kim didn't do what?" Kimberly asked, walking into the kitchen.

"Tell Cesare how Judith likes her coffee," Sandra said.

"Do I know how Jude likes her coffee?" Kimberly wrinkled her nose.

I sat back, puzzlement setting in with a vengeance. "But if you guys didn't tell him, how would he have known?"

"Coincidence?" Sandra suggested.

"Like the rope and drowning child were coincidence?" I countered. "It's not like he's a mind-reader, right?"

Sandra snorted at the absurdity of my statement.

"Probably not." Kimberly shrugged. "But imagine how cool it would be if he was."

"Don't make me have this conversation again, Kim. Magic isn't real." Sandra gave one of her signature sighs.

"Well, of course, magic isn't real to those who don't believe—"

"You have *got* to stop—"

"Ladies!" That was me.

Honestly.

Hanging out with these two was getting harder and harder.

Sandra crossed her arms "There is no magic here, Kim. Cesare must simply be observant. It's not like we haven't had coffee with him before. End of story."

Hmmmm, but was it? I wasn't sure.

One more thing to add to the list.

Now Cesare had to spill the beans (pun intended) as to how he had learned my coffee preferences.

AFTER BREAKFAST AND LISTENING TO another three debates between Sandra and Kimberly about the boys they were meeting up with for lunch, I decided to go in search of Cesare.

He didn't answer the door when I knocked on his apartment, nor was he in his offices on the ground floor. Part of me was surprised that he would disappear so completely without at least leaving a message, particularly after our conversation the day before.

I was standing in the stairwell, dithering whether or not to leave Cesare a note, when his mother's apartment door opened.

"*Ciao, bellina.*" She stood with a hand on the door frame, immaculately dressed with her dark hair cut into a stylish bob. The resemblance to Cesare was faint but there. "*Vieni.*" She beckoned with one hand. "Come."

I smiled and followed her up the few stairs and into her apartment.

I had met Cesare's mother in passing several times. He had introduced us that first day and she had seemed unfailingly kind. But given her limited understanding of English and my very rudimentary Italian, talking with each other was difficult.

I gathered that Cesare's father was no longer in the picture. Of course, now that I knew Cesare was an earl, that had to mean that his father was no longer living, as the title had passed to his son.

Logic again.

I wanted to ask Cesare about it. Was his father dead? How had he died? And how had Cesare and his mother dealt with his loss?

I stood in the long hallway as she shut the door behind us, surreptitiously studying her apartment; it appeared to be a copy of ours upstairs.

"I am sorry I don't speak much Italian, Mrs. D'Angelo," I said to her as she turned around.

She waved a hand. "*Non m'importa,*" she said, which I took to mean she was okay with it.

She motioned for me to pass into her living room, a larger space with huge windows and a beautiful frescoed ceiling.

"I'm Judith, by the way." I stuck out my hand to her. "I don't know if you remember."

She smiled and took my hand. "Alice."

It was only later that I learned she spelled her name the same as the English *Alice*. She pronounced it differently, however: ah-LEE-chay.

I sat on the couch. She took a chair opposite me.

"Thank you for letting us stay." I said the words slowly, hoping that might help her understand. I also pointed at the ceiling in case she missed what I was saying.

"*Figurati,*" she replied. "It iza nothing." Her English was heavily accented but still understandable.

We stared at each other awkwardly for a moment.

I got the sense that she was assessing me, weighing my presence in her son's life. Part of me expected her to be wary. I was a foreigner and she knew nothing about me. But, instead, I would have labeled her emotion as poignant or even compassionate.

But my brain told me that was weird, so I dismissed the thought. Why would Cesare's mother look at me compassionately?

"Do you know where Cesare is?" I asked.

"*Cesare non si sente bene oggi,*" she replied before pausing, thinking. "Cesare . . . he iza sick."

"Oh. Poor guy."

That explained it, I supposed. He had seemed fine the night before, but a stomach bug or something could come on quickly.

Or, thinking back to his odd seizures, he could be more seriously ill.

"May I see him? Can I help?"

Alice looked at me blankly. I scrambled trying to think of the right word. What had Cesare said at the market when we needed help?

"Cesare," I tried again. "*Aiuto?*"

"Oh, no, no." Alice shook her finger. "*Lui sta male oggi, ma non c'è niente da fare. Lui sarà meglio domani.*"

I froze. I had no idea what she had just said.

Alice sighed and cocked her head, thinking. "Tomorrow. Cesare be better."

Okay, I could live with that.

We stared at each other awkwardly again. I got the feeling that Alice wanted to ask me questions, but the language proved an impossible barrier.

My eye snagged on a series of photos atop a hutch along one wall. They featured a younger version of Alice with a man who bore a strong resemblance to Cesare. Cesare's father, I assumed.

"Your husband?" I asked, pointing to the photos. "Uhmm . . . Cesare. Father?"

Alice followed my finger. "*Sì, quello è mio marito.* My husband."

I smiled. "Handsome."

Alice matched my grin. "*Sì, lui era molto bello.*"

The photos moved through Cesare's childhood, too, as he joined the family. There were photos of them skiing in Switzerland, visiting the Tower of London, standing in front of an old Italian villa, sailing aboard a small yacht.

But by the time Cesare was a teenager, the photos depicted just Cesare and Alice. Was that when Cesare's father had died? The man had to have been quite young.

I pointed between two photos, one showing the three of them together and another with just Alice and Cesare. "What happened to him?" I pointed back to her husband.

I had to know. It seemed important somehow.

Alice made a face. "*Cesare non te l'ha detto?*"

I froze. I had no idea what she had just said.

She paused, thinking.

"Cesare . . . he telled you?" she asked.

"Told me?" I shook my head. "No, Cesare has not told me. What happened?"

Alice frowned, face puzzled. "*Non c'è per me parlarne.*" Another pause. "I cannot say."

Now it was my turn to look puzzled. What couldn't she say?

She shook her head and pointed to her husband. "*Lui è morto.*"

He is dead. That I understood.

Alice gave me a sad, apologetic kinda smile.

I excused myself a moment later, catching up with Kimberly and Sandra who were shopping in the street markets around San Lorenzo.

All the while, thoughts of Cesare continued to bombard me. How had his father died? Was Cesare really and truly sick?

And what, if anything, was I going to do about the convergence of Steve, fear, kisses and the longing that Cesare D'Angelo created?

THE NEXT SEVEN WEEKS PLAYED LIKE a montage sequence from an old-fashioned romance film. Think *Roman Holiday* or *Breakfast at Tiffany's*.

And, okay, maybe I had a bit of a thing for Audrey Hepburn.

I spent time with Cesare. I traveled around Europe with Kimberly and Sandra.

Years later, bits and pieces of those weeks would click through my brain. Like Cesare's polaroids sliding in and out of consciousness.

Small snapshots of memory frozen in time.

Click.

Cesare bending down to me, the sun threading through his dark hair, whispering how beautiful I looked.

Click.

Kimberly, Sandra and I running up a hill outside Salzburg, spinning like idiots, laughing ourselves sick trying to recreate the opening sequence of *The Sound of Music*.

Click.

All of us seated at the dining table in Alice's apartment, talking over dinner, Cesare meeting my eyes with a wink.

Click.

Kimberly and I rolling our eyes behind Sandra's back as she haggled for a solid hour with street vendors near the Berlin Wall.

Click.

Me stepping off the train in central Florence, astonished to find Cesare waiting for me with a bouquet of peonies.

Click. Click. Click.

Through it all, I felt like I was coming to know Cesare deeply and, yet, not at all.

I knew tiny details—like how he hated *Dynasty*, but secretly enjoyed

The Love Boat, or that he detested the texture of custards and puddings—but I still didn't know any of the big stuff.

Like how and when his father had died? Or why Cesare was called the Damned Earl and why couldn't he tell me the story behind it? Or what was up with his continued seizures? Clearly he was an epileptic of some sort, at the very least, but he kept insisting the seizures were nothing to worry about.

I also didn't know what to make of Cesare's almost extrasensory ability to anticipate when things were going to happen.

Certain events stood out:

Cesare casually opening an umbrella as we stood downtown on a sunny day, raising it over my head just in time to prevent pigeon poop from landing in my hair.

Cesare abruptly stretching his arm out to his side and, half-a-second later, backhandedly catching a child who tumbled off a stone wall.

But one thing was clear:

I was falling hard for Cesare D'Angelo.

SOMETIMES BIG DECISIONS ARE MOMENTOUS. They come with angels singing and hosannas and lightning claps of astonished wonder.

Other times, life-altering decisions start as a trickle of thought that slips by barely noticed, growing so slowly into a flood until one minute you're sitting eating a *pain au chocolat* along the Seine in Paris with your friends and the next you're painfully aware you will never marry Steve.

"I'm never going to marry Steve," I said the words aloud, staring across the river to the Cathedral of Notre Dame. Kimberly sat beside me, both of us eating pastries while we waited for Sandra to finish chatting about coffee with a barista across the street.

"Well, duh," Kimberly replied without missing a beat, finishing off her *profiterole* with a delighted moan.

I frowned and looked at her. "What's that supposed to mean?"

She shrugged, licking custard off her fingers. "Just what I said. Duh. Of course you're not going to marry Steve."

"Because you think I'm going to marry Cesare?"

"Not necessarily. Sure, the chemistry between you and Cesare is hella-hot, but that doesn't mean you two are gonna get hitched."

"Well, then, how can you say that I won't ever marry Steve?"

"Because you clearly don't love him."

"He's my boyfriend—"

"No, he's the boring on-a-break guy that you call a boyfriend because you're too afraid to embrace the chaos of messier feelings."

Whoa.

Kimberly's look said she was sorry but not really.

This was the thing with Kimberly. She was generally flighty and a lot ditzy, so when she made a profound observation, it really jarred me. But when she *did* say those deeper things, she was almost always right.

Again, another reason why we were friends.

And with this . . . she *was* right.

I was afraid to break up with Steve. Not because I was worried about what he would say or how I would act.

No. I was afraid because I didn't know what came *after* breaking up with Steve. After Steve stretched with blank unknown-ness.

But the thought of moving Cesare from the Never column to the Possible one in my mental list of Men I Might End Up Marrying . . .

That was absolutely terrifying.

Not because I didn't want it. But because I maybe wanted it too much, and I intuitively understood the enormous upheaval a life with Cesare would bring.

The man was a freakin' earl, for heaven's sake, not to mention he lived in Italy, had weird seizures and obviously kept secrets from me.

So . . . I had no clue what to do about Cesare.

But I did know things were over with Steve.

Kimberly and I stared at the Seine as it rolled along, the sluggish green-brown water eddying around the boats moored along its sides.

"I really like Cesare," I said.

"Again . . . duh," Kimberly snorted.

"I'm probably half-way to being in love with him."

"You're way past half-way."

"You think?" I shot her a glance. "How do you know if you're in love? Like, for reals?"

"It's simple." Kimberly shrugged. "You just ask yourself: Do I love him? If you don't immediately shout, YES!, then you're not in love."

A pause.

"That's the stupidest explanation of love I've ever heard." I shook my head.

"No, it's really not. Do you love Steve?"

I thought for a second. "Maybe. Possibly at one point. I honestly don't know."

"Mmmmm, follow-up question. Do you love your mom?"

"Of course."

"Your sister?"

"Duh."

Kimberly swept her hand, palm up, in an arc in front of her. "I rest my case."

I made a face at her. "You *have* to love your family. It doesn't work that way with romantic love. It's not the same thing."

Kimberly shot me an oh-you-sweet-naive-idiot look. "It's exactly the same thing. Someday, you'll know what I mean."

I was reserving judgment. Not all of us were touchy-feely artsy people. Sometimes love was as much a choice as a feeling.

Wait. I needed to say that.

"Sometimes love is a choice."

"I don't disagree." Kimberly nodded, pondering the idea. "But romantic love will always defy logic. Sometimes with romantic love, you wake up one morning and you just *know*—you love this person and you never want to be apart from them. It's the nature of it."

We sat in silence for a moment.

Traffic rushed behind us. A tour boat moved sluggishly up the river, tourists snapping photos, flashes popping in the bright sunlight.

"I guess I should call Steve and break up with him."

"About time."

"I don't know what to do about Cesare. Even if we fall in love, it's not like I'm going to give up my career in the States to stay here with him."

"I wouldn't worry too much about that. If it's right, you guys will find a way."

Kimberly looked over her shoulder at our friend, finally crossing the street to us. "Do you think Sandra will ever open a coffee shop?"

"Knowing Sandra? Of course. It's just a question of how quickly she makes her first million."

MY BREAK-UP WITH STEVE WAS comically painful.

Because why would something like that be easy and graceful when it could be agonizingly awkward?

The sound delay over the phone line was a solid ten seconds, causing our sentences to overlap in tortuous ways, each of us replying to what the other said two sentences before.

But after three minutes of talking over one another with "Hey" and "Whoops, sorry" and "No, you go first," we finally managed to get to the point, though the delay remained:

Me: "Steve, I have something I need to talk to you about."

Steve: "I'm so glad you called. It's nice to hear your voice."

Me: "I've been thinking about us a lot lately."

Steve: "I enjoy talking to you, too, babe."

Me: "So . . . I want to make our break permanent."

Steve: "I've been thinking about us, too, and wondering if you want to go ring shopping when you get home."

Ouch.

Yeah.

Things sorta went downhill from there.

Steve was not happy.

I cried afterward.

Not because I was upset over the decision. But more because there were so many emotions in my chest—fear, worry, excitement, insecurity—that crying seemed the easiest way to get them all out.

I hadn't broken up with Steve because I wanted Cesare more. I wasn't dumping one guy to take on another.

No, it was more that the bright color and vivid living I felt with Cesare illuminated the lack of those things in my relationship with Steve. Regardless of what happened with Cesare, my relationship with Steve was over.

I didn't love Steve. I cared about him as a friend but nothing more.

Despite what Kimberly had said, understanding love was not simple. You didn't just wake up and *know* that you were in love with someone.

I wasn't sure if I understood exactly what love was. And I didn't know if the achy, jittery feeling constricting my chest every time I thought of Cesare was the beginnings of love, but I needed more time to find out.

I wanted to be with someone who demanded all my kisses.

I wanted that person to be Cesare D'Angelo.

I arrived back in Florence practically vibrating with my need to talk to Cesare about decisions and Steve and, well . . . things.

Mostly kissing things.

Lots and lots of kissing things.

All the kissing things.

The train ride home from Paris had been hours of wondering how Cesare would react to my news.

I crashed through the front door of our apartment and had myself showered and primped and cutely attired in record time.

I bounced down the stairs to Cesare's apartment. My heart danced in my chest, clogging my throat with excitement.

Did I just come right out and tell him that I had broken up with Steve? Or did I ease into it?

And after telling him about Steve, how should I move to kissing? We hadn't spoken about kissing since that day at San Marco. So would I have to bring it up again?

Or would Cesare's eyes widen with overjoyed wonder at the news, compelling him to gather me into his arms, pressing me against the wall and kissing me senseless?

Yum.

Please.

Let's do that last one.

I stopped in front of Cesare's apartment door and smoothed the front of my kicky skirt.

Deep breath.

I knocked on his door.

The sounds of shuffling and then the door opened and there he was.

Right in front of me.

He froze at the sight of me, eyes flaring wide.

But I couldn't focus on his reaction. I was too lost in him: the simple white t-shirt pulling on his deep chest, loose blue jeans, dark scruff on his chin, hair askew.

Wow.

I had only been gone five days, but it felt like months. Like I was seeing him shiny and new, and I really liked what I saw.

Abruptly, I was tongue-tied and unsure.

"Hey," I said breathlessly.

Yeah, that was the best greeting my stunned brain could come up with.

"Hi!" he replied.

His voice was bright, but was it *too* bright? Was he happy to see me? Or simply surprised?

"I didn't know you would be back so soon," he continued.

Okay, so I was going with surprised then. But his tone was more than just surprised. It was almost as if he were *upset* that he hadn't known.

I rocked on my heels. "Yeah, we just got in. I couldn't wait to see you."

He smiled, slow and sexy. He braced an arm against the doorjamb, the movement doing amazing things for the muscles I could see moving in his upper body.

My eyes darted to his lush mouth.

Almost involuntarily, I found myself leaning in his direction.

"So, uhm, I have some good news." I licked my bottom lip. His eyes followed the motion of my tongue.

"You do?" He canted toward me.

This was good. This was very good. I could almost feel his kissable lips on mine.

"Yeah." I swallowed. *Just tell him already*. "I broke up with Steve."

In my nervous haste, I said the words too fast: *IbrokeupwithSteve*.

He blinked, his head tilting back. A frown appeared. "What? What did you say?"

Deep breath.

"I broke up with Steve," I repeated more clearly.

Silence.

Cesare stared at me, expression frozen.

Uhm, okay.

I hadn't been a hundred percent sure what his reaction would be, but stunned silence had *not* been on my list.

Maybe he didn't understand what I meant by that? I didn't know, but I was so nervous, I couldn't seem to stop my mouth from talking.

And so I rambled on. "I didn't break up with Steve because of you. But I've been thinking a lot about what you said, how you're a stingy kisser and I realized that I want to be with someone who is a stingy kisser; someone who values me and values themselves and doesn't just see me as a way to pass time but as a real person"—*you've got to stop talking*—"and I want to be the real person for you. I want to be the one who gets all your kisses . . ."

I was breathless and whispering by the end.

As I had spoken, all the color had drained from Cesare's face. If I had been any less nervous and flustered, I might have been alarmed.

He swallowed, Adam's apple bobbing up and down.

He shook his head once, twice.

"I—" He stopped, pinched his lips together, shook his head. "You've surprised me. This is . . . this is . . . unexpected."

Again, he sounded puzzled by that, as if being surprised was something unusual for him. Like he should have *known* this conversation was coming.

But that thought was ridiculous. No one can know the future.

His gaze turned inward, his chest heaved, almost as if he were having to swallow back a panic attack. Like me coming to him with these words was at once unimaginable joy and brutal agony and he didn't know how to process it.

Or maybe he just really didn't like being surprised with things outside his control.

Regardless . . . the worst thing happened—

Cesare turned around.

Walked back into his apartment.

And. Shut. The. Door.

. . .

. . .

. . .

So . . . that just happened.

I stared down his closed door, trying to process the last three minutes.

I was pretty sure my jaw had officially hit the floor.

A few of my thoughts in no particular order:

Wow. That was unexpected for me, too.

What have we been doing for the past—how long has it been?—seven weeks?

He doesn't want my kisses.

Oh no. I'm going to cry over this.

What. The. Hell?!

How dare he?

Don'tcrydon'tcrydon'tcry.

I tapped my foot, biting my lip, trying to decide what to do.

Storm in there and pound my fists on his damned-earl chest until he cried for mercy and talked to me?

Round up Kimberly and Sandra and head out of town?

Drown my sorrows in too much gelato and carb-laden pasta?

I stood there for what felt like an hour but was probably only a minute, vacillating between all three when the door swung open again.

Cesare was back.

Boy . . . was he ever back.

Every last ounce of his indecision had vanished. Whatever emotion had seized him just moments before was utterly gone.

His eyes devoured me. Hungry. Intent.

Feral.

Whoa.

I took a step back. "You shut the door in my face." The words flew from my mouth.

He matched my step, coming toward me. "I'm sorry, *tesora mia*. You surprised me. I'm not used to being surprised."

"That's no excuse." I took another step back.

"You're right." Another step forward. "It is no excuse." Another step. "I'm going to have to make it up to you."

He didn't sound like that would be a chore.

I took another step back, but my heels encountered the wall opposite his door.

Cesare kept coming until every last inch of his oh-so-fine body was pressed against mine and he was all I could see. One hand cupped my face, the other snaked around my waist.

I had no choice but to wrap my arms around his shoulders.

"Last chance," he growled.

I repeat—

He. Growled.

"Uhmmm . . . last chance for a kiss?" Who knew my voice could sound so breathless?

"No. Last chance for you to run."

"Run?" Yep. Still breathless.

It was just . . . he was so here and present and whydoeshehavetosmellsogood?

"I told you . . . that first day at the Uffizi, that I would bring you heartache. That, if you were smart, you would run from me."

Wow. That was some extremely good recall he had going on there.

My breath hiccupped in my chest. My arms clenched around him convulsively.

No!

The thought was instant and based on instinct.

I would *not* run from him.

Was this the reason for his earlier reaction? That he saw himself as broken?

"Why? Why should I run?"

"I'll bring you grief."

"Why do you say that?"

"It's the truth."

"You don't know that."

"What if I do?"

My tone morphed into exasperation. "Everything is 'what if'? What if we die on the way home today? What if the world is destroyed by an asteroid tomorrow? What if I live to be a hundred? There are no guarantees in life. Only probabilities."

Silence.

He continued to breathe me in.

"What if the probability is high that I will cause you heartache?" he finally asked.

I paused . . . but I already knew the answer.

"Heartache is my choice. The pain of heartbreak is always the risk of caring for someone. I appreciate you being upfront with me, but the choice is mine. Do you choose me?" I asked.

"Yes." His eyes darted to my lips. "Emphatically, yes."

"What if I break *your* heart, huh?"

"Not going to happen."

"Cocky."

"No. Truth."

A beat.

"Well," I said on a whisper, "I choose *this*."

I leaned into him and brushed my lips over his ear.

My touch jolted him, snapping something. I felt the current shoot through his body, his arms tightening reflexively, clutching me that much closer.

Cesare sealed his mouth over mine. No hesitation. No doubt. Eager. Seeking.

He tasted of excitement and comfort and yearning and promise.

For my part, I was boneless delight. More goosebump than skin. Starved and feasting.

His hands were helpless to remain still. They roamed my back, one threading into my hair. He kissed me, over and over. Every time I pulled back, he chased my mouth, demanding more.

Not that I minded.

Cesare D'Angelo was *finally* kissing me. And I wanted more and more.

I wanted all his kisses.

Nothing in my previous twenty-six years of life had prepared me for the sheer *rightness* of kissing him.

He was home. It was that simple.

We kissed for eons there in the stairwell. Galaxies were born. Entire solar systems came and went. The world went supernova.

Eventually, Cesare pulled back, stroking a finger down my cheek. He looked at me intently, as if memorizing my face. I labeled the look his 'Intense Stare,' and decided it made me feel like I was sun to his night.

I tugged him in for another kiss.

"Ya know, when you want a girl to run, you shouldn't kiss her quite so well," I murmured against his lips.

"I didn't say I *wanted* you to run," he returned. "But my conscience felt like you should be warned."

"I appreciate your conscience's concern, but I've never been better." Truth.

He pecked my mouth again, lingering.

"Come with me tomorrow," he said.

"Okay."

He huffed a laugh. "Just like that? You agree? No hesitation? Where is the logical woman I met all those weeks ago?"

"You pushed her out of her rigid shell," I chuckled. "You only have yourself to blame."

"*Cara mia*, I will always blame myself," was his cryptic reply.

I should have told him right then that I would never blame him. That I truly chose this. That he was never to shoulder the burden of my non-existent regret.

But instead I kissed him and dreamed of our golden tomorrow.

C esare owned a motorcycle.

I mean, *of course*, he would own a motorcycle. The powerful machine fit him somehow.

But . . . he had seriously been holding out on me.

First kisses and now hot motorbike rides.

After an extremely delightful evening kissing and cuddling, I had risen the next morning to find Cesare waiting with a picnic basket and helmet.

His words? "I thought we could get outside Florence and visit some of Tuscany."

The words themselves were fantastic.

Yes, please.

What woman wouldn't melt into a puddle of gooey adoration at the thought of having a romantic picnic with a gorgeous Italian hunk?

The problem? Despite us having locked lips for hours the night before, Cesare's behavior toward me hadn't changed much.

I hadn't thought through precisely *what* his behavior should be the morning after declaring I wanted all his kisses, but I had expected the two of us would feel more . . . relationship-ish. That he would greet me with a passionate kiss or a heated look or *something*.

Instead, I got a chaste peck on the cheek and friendly smile, i.e. how Cesare always greeted me.

I wasn't sure what to make of it. Clearly we were in the middle of that awkward I-think-we're-in-a-relationship-but-I'm-not-entirely-sure stage. I had kinda assumed that when Cesare said he wanted all my kisses that meant we would be an item. But now . . . I wasn't quite so sure.

I hesitated to label my emotions for Cesare as love, but I was positive they were more than like or friendship or admiration or respect or adoration, but instead, some potent mixture of all of them.

Was that love? I didn't know.

Regardless, I cared too much about this man to not say something. I intended to talk to him about us, but tucked tight up against Cesare on the back of his motorcycle was not the time or place.

We zoomed through traffic, buzzing around Piazza Santa Croce and then the crush of buses and taxis circling the Duomo before moving past the enormous *Fortezza da Basso*, a fourteenth century fortress just outside downtown. We crossed over the Arno and melted into the hills south of Florence.

There is nothing quite like whizzing past olive orchards and vineyards and rolling Tuscan hills on a motorcycle. Wind tugged at my hair as I breathed in deep gulps of fresh, country air. Fluffy clouds dotted the blue sky like so many sheep.

For the record, riding a motorcycle with Cesare wasn't quite as exhilarating as a make-out session, but it was a strong second place.

Eventually, we climbed a steep hill to a walled, medieval-looking city, towers peeking above the stone ramparts. Cesare parked his bike in the dusty piazza in front of the main city gate.

I peeled myself off his body, staggering a little as I stepped off the bike. I had been holding on tight for well over an hour.

"This town is gorgeous. Where are we?" I asked as I threaded my fingers through my hair, trying to tame it back down.

"San Gimignano." Cesare unstrapped our lunch from the back of the bike, stealing glances at me.

Stealing glances was good. Though, quite frankly, he could steal a kiss or two.

That said, I was grateful I had dressed for the kill—a silky white shirt with the ends tied at my waist; thigh-skimming, high-waisted denim shorts; white high-top sneakers; hair wild and curly.

Granted, the loose hair had proved a problem on the motorcycle, but as Cesare kept staring at me from the corner of his eye, it was worth it.

"What makes this place special? I mean, it looks amazing, but why did you choose it?" I asked, continuing to mess with my hair. Cesare obliged and continued to stare, his eyes getting lost in me over and over.

I was vain enough to find it gratifying.

But his mood was still decidedly . . . off. His shoulders were stiff and his smiles didn't quite reach his eyes. He appeared . . . tense. Which seemed the wrong emotion entirely.

Was he already regretting his behavior from the night before?

My heart choked me at the thought of all my fervent feelings for him being unrequited. Figured that when I finally felt something that might be moving from deep-crush to actual love, it turned out to be the unrequited variety.

Definitely needed to have that conversation.

Cesare finally swallowed, shaking his head as if trying to free cobwebs. "There is something magical about San Gimignano. The city was once a rival of Siena and Florence itself. Around eight hundred years ago, all three cities were around the same size. But the plague in the fourteenth century hit San Gimignano particularly hard, and the city never really recovered. Instead, it remained frozen in time."

"Wow. So it hasn't changed much since the 1350s?"

"Exactly. It's like a living time machine. But more importantly for me, my ancestors come from San Gimignano. When I visit, I am reminded of where it all began."

At the time, I assumed he meant 'where his family began' but that wasn't entirely it.

Instead, I simply replied: "How awesome. Show me the city."

And let me find a good opening to ask why you're acting like nothing has changed between us.

Snagging our picnic basket in one hand and my fingers with his other, Cesare led me through the city gates and up a cobblestone street lined with medieval storefronts.

Weaving our way through tourists, hand-in-hand, was delightfully boyfriend/girlfriend-ish, but the street was decidedly crowded. So about midway up, Cesare turned up an alleyway to the left, leading me up stairs and through several narrow passageways between houses. Eventually, we stumbled out into an open courtyard and then across it into a walled area.

"This is the *fortezza*, the old castle," Cesare explained as I took in the open space.

Wild roses spilled over the tumbled stones and wisteria roses climbed up the tower walls. Grass grew tall on the ground. Fortunately, few tourists had wandered this far away from the central streets.

We had the fortress essentially to ourselves. Definitely a good place to air my questions.

"Cesare—" I began.

But he was still talking. "You can see the tower ruins there and there." He pointed to the circular walls that projected outward, looming overhead. "Now it's just a hollow ruin."

"Yes, it's a beautiful ruin," I said. "Sometimes broken things are more beautiful because of their brokenness, not in spite of it."

I said the words casually, looking for another opening to change the topic to us, but given how Cesare froze, his gaze morphed instantly into his characteristic mix of melancholy affection, understanding blazed through me.

Was his hesitation today more of his sense of brokenness? Was that why he was acting weird? No, not weird . . .

Distant. He was distant.

I had been obsessing over him pulling away from me, but what if it were the opposite? What if he was waiting for me to show that I was comfortable with the change in our relationship? What if all his tension was insecurity? Like he was waiting for the other shoe to drop, for me to decide I didn't want to be with him or something.

As if I were that fickle.

There was only one way to test my theory.

Without thinking, I stepped closer to him, slipping an arm around his waist. I seemed helpless to *not* touch him. He watched me through hooded eyes, setting our picnic on the ground and sliding a hand around my back, pulling me into him.

I rested my hands on his shoulders, tucking my nose into his neck.

This.

This was what I wanted.

Cesare and I . . . together.

Part of me stood back in wonder, surprised that my coolly logical self could have fallen so far. My behavior and thoughts were emotional and irrational and I didn't do emotional and irrational.

But the rest of me cared too deeply for Cesare to mind. I could hardly think past the longing thrumming through me.

He pulled me closer and sighed into my ear, a sound of deep contentment.

"What's wrong?" I murmured in his ear.

"Nothing is wrong when I'm holding you, *cara.*"

"Cesare." Warning in my tone. I tightened my grip on him. "You know that's not what I meant."

He simply hummed and nuzzled my neck with his nose.

Men!

I blurted it all out. "I tell you I want all your kisses—and I do, that hasn't changed—and you kiss me and it's wonderful but then today you're distant and now I'm confused because I thought kissing would mean something to you, because it definitely means something to me, and I want our relationship to feel like more than friendship, because I think it *is* more than simple friendship. Basically, I miss you and want us to feel more . . . together."

I swallowed. I hadn't intended to lay it all on the line so bluntly, but my heart ran away with my mouth.

It didn't help that Cesare paused as I talked, pulling his head upright and staring at me.

That wonderful intensity returned to his hazel eyes. He lifted both hands and cradled my face, his eyes roaming my face, gaze alight with what I wanted to call *adoration*.

What was up with his hot and cold behavior?

I was so confused.

So I said as much.

"Cesare, I'm so confused. What's going on?"

He shook his head and then gently shook mine, as he still held my cheeks. I wrapped my hands around his wrists.

"*Never* doubt my devotion to you, Judith Campbell. I'm sorry for my behavior today. I guess . . ." He paused, looked away and then came back to me. "I guess I just can't believe that you're here, in my arms, saying these things to me. It feels like some fantastical dream. You had Steve and so I had assumed that nothing would happen between us. That we would only remain in possibility. But then last night and now—" He swallowed, that same adoration shining through. "—I guess I'm just nervous. I care so deeply for you and I desperately want you to stay in my life, but I have things to tell you that are . . . difficult."

He gave me a small smile that didn't quite reach his eyes.

My heart was a kettle drum in my chest. Now *I* was nervous. What did he need to tell me? Was I finally going to learn all his secrets? What if I didn't like what I learned?

"Okay, let's talk. Is this about your seizures?"

He nodded. "Among other things."

"Will you answer my questions?"

"Yes." No hesitation.

"*All* my questions."

"Yes."

"I have a lot of questions."

"I have years of time."

"Wow! So, let's get start—"

Shouting and loud laughter interrupted us. A group of rowdy teenagers filtered into the far side of the fortress ruins, yelling and kicking up dust. We both looked at them.

Cesare took advantage of my turned head to brush a kiss across my cheek before pulling entirely away.

I missed him almost instantly.

He clearly understood the petulant frown on my face.

"I don't know how much quiet we're going to get here and this will take a while." He hefted the picnic basket. "I know of a secluded place where we can eat lunch and chat."

I looked at the hamper. My nerves were jittery. "I'm good. Let's just skip to chatting."

He paused. "No, you have to eat, *cara mia*. Let me feed you first."

"But I have so many questions!"

"Eat, *cara*," he chuckled, adoringly. "I packed all this for you. Choose something. You can eat while we walk, and I'll tell you about San Gimignano."

"I want to hear about you, though."

"It's all related, *cara*. Trust me. Eat."

Cesare opened the picnic basket. I glimpsed sandwiches, apples, grapes and a package of something wrapped in brown paper.

I took a pile of grapes and nodded at Cesare to lead the way. We wandered down into town, me munching on grapes—the huge, old-school kind with peppery seeds in the middle. Narrow, medieval streets bled into each other, ancient arches spanning the roads here and there.

My mind was in upheaval. Cesare would answer all my questions, but the answers were 'difficult,' he said. It had to do with his health, I was sure, those odd seizures.

As we walked, Cesare talked about San Gimignano. The needed backstory, I guess?

San Gimignano was once known as the city of a thousand towers. There probably weren't ever a thousand, but given how many still stood, there might have been close to a hundred once. I asked him about his family connection to the city.

"My family has lived here since ancient times. D'Angelo is an old, venerated name, so who knows when they first came to San Gimignano. As the city dates to the Etruscan era, before the Romans arrived, my ancestors could have been here for thousands of years. Records begin in earnest in the early Middle Ages, about the time of Dante Alighieri around 1200."

"Were you earls even then?" I asked.

"No, that came much later. During the Middle Ages, the D'Angelos were wealthy merchants. Not part of the ultra-wealthy elite, but moneyed enough that they had a seat on the local ruling council."

"The ruling council?"

We walked out from a dark tunnel into one of the main piazzas, an enormous ancient well in the middle.

"Yeah, each of these little hilltop towns was basically a democratic oligarchy, ruled by an elected mayor—a *podestà*, as he was known—who settled disputes. But then around 1275, Giovanni D'Angelo decided to improve his family's fortune. He made a series of wise investments, outsmarted his rivals and became fabulously wealthy." He handed me a sandwich—meat wrapped in a ciabatta roll, just like I like it.

"He must have been quite the remarkable guy." I unwrapped my sandwich.

Cesare snorted. "Something like that. His ambition is not disputed." He said the words almost bitterly, which was odd.

But as I had just taken a bite of the most delicious sandwich ever, all follow-up questions scattered.

"Oh my gosh!" I may have moaned a little and the words came out more like 'Uh ma gof' with my mouth full.

But . . . oh my gosh! The sandwich was so good.

The perfect blend of salty meat, smooth cheese, a drizzle of olive oil, a hint of spicy mustard, all tucked into bread that was at once soft and spongy and deliciously chewy.

Cesare had knocked it out of the park.

"You like?" he asked.

I nodded, taking another eager bite.

We continued to walk through the town, me savoring my

sandwich—seriously, it was so exactly perfect to my tastes—and Cesare talking about the town. Eventually, we moved off the beaten tourist path and passed through a back city gate, walking down a steep, cobblestone street. This road was clearly not traveled much, given the moss and grass poking up between the stones. It curved around the outside of the city.

At the bottom of the steep road, a medieval-era structure stood, partially built into the side of the hill. The front of the building featured a sequence of arches atop a wide wall about three feet high. Inside, water bubbled and flowed through a series of man-made pools.

Opposite the arches and water, a low stone fence separated the lane from a drop to the countryside below. Panoramic views of the Tuscan countryside extended into the far distance.

The entire setting was exquisite: incredible vista; gurgling, crystal clear water; ancient arches covered in vines and moss; birds chirping and, best of all, not another soul in sight.

Perfect for a long chat.

I was a bundle of nerves, completely keyed up. Idea after idea careened through my mind, each more random than the last.

I brushed away the crumbs from the last of my sandwich and pointed at the odd, arched enclosure. "What's this place?"

Cesare stopped beside me. "They're called *fonti mediovali*—which loosely translated means 'medieval sources' or springs. There isn't really a word in English for what they are, but they were a sort of communal well. Basically, each one of these Tuscan hilltop towns had *fonti*, a series of man-made pools that they used for drinking water, washing and watering animals."

I climbed atop the low wall under one of the arches, touching a hand to the clear, cold water. The pools extended the entire length of the enclosure, each running into the next. Ancient, carved columns and arches supported the barrel vault roof.

Magical seemed an understatement.

Two minutes later, I had my shoes off and was sitting on the wide ledge, sinking my feet into the blessed coolness.

"Can we please talk now?" I asked.

"Yes."

Cesare joined me, pulling off his shoes and cuffing his pants.

"Spill." I beckoned with my fingers. "Or should I just start asking questions?"

"Let me go first. Here, you can have some of these while I talk."

He unwrapped the final brown package from our picnic basket, revealing half-moon circles of what looked like raisin-filled cookies, just like my grandma used to make.

Huh. I had no idea Italians ate cookies like that, too.

I hadn't had a cookie like this since Grandma had passed away six years ago. They were too time consuming to make and the one time I had tried, I had made a mess of it. Grandma hadn't written down her recipe, unfortunately, and I couldn't figure out how to give the filling her signature tangy punch while keeping the crust flaky.

Cesare offered one to me, as if the cookies were important somehow.

Smiling, I bit into it. Flavor and texture exploded in my mouth—tartly sweet filling inside and crumbly cookie outside.

Tears instantly swamped me.

The cookies weren't just similar to my grandma's—they were carbon copies.

Identical in every way.

What were the chances?

The familiar taste sent me hurtling back in time, to sitting in my grandma's kitchen, listening to her tell stories of how she met my grandpa while we filled cookies together.

Man, I missed her.

Crazy how a taste or a smell can catapult you into memory like that, wiping every other thought from your mind.

I swiped at my cheeks, eating another bite or two.

I finally thought to glance at Cesare. I expected him to ask me what was wrong or at least comment on my obvious emotional issues.

But instead he simply stared at me with what could only be called . . . *knowing*. As if he had *known* the cookies would bring back a flood of memories.

Which seemed . . . impossible.

But then, it also seemed improbable that he would have cookies that were identical to those my grandma made me as a child.

Or that he would know exactly how I prefer my coffee.

Or that he would know he needed a rope to pull a small child from a river before the accident even happened.

Or all the other little things he had known over the past weeks.

My heartbeat thundered in my ears.

I kept my eyes on him, licking a few crumbs from my mouth.

"Did you know?" I had to ask it. I pointed to my half-eaten cookie. "Did you know that these would remind me of my grandma?"

The fact that he didn't look confused or surprised was all the confirmation I needed.

Goosebumps scattered down my arms. I shook my head, the silence stretching.

There are certain moments in your life where you know you sit on a precipice. That the entire course of your existence hangs in the balance. Where shock and surprise etch every little detail deep into memory.

The lazy buzz of cicadas. The barely-there wind tugging at my hair. The lingering smell of woodsmoke. The cooler, mossy air threading around me from the *fonti*.

Even years later, I would be able to bring up every tiny nuance of that moment.

Cesare stared at me with those hazel eyes of his, earnest and pleading, begging me to accept and understand what he was going to say.

"What's going on here, Cesare?" I licked my lips again. "What do you need to tell me?"

Each answer I could think of defied logic. Cesare continued to look at me with that same melancholy understanding.

My mind raced, trying desperately to connect the dots, understand all the data points he had fed me.

"This is starting to freak me out." I set the cookie aside, wiping my hands on my shorts. "Do you have a stalking fetish? Did you call my family and get my grandma's recipe?"

"No. Nothing like that."

"Do you know my family?" I asked.

"No."

"So what is it?" My heart plummeted. "You said earlier that your seizures were part of it. Do you have a brain tumor or something?"

Though I didn't see how a brain tumor helped him know how I liked my coffee.

Cesare shook his head. "You have to know, before I begin, that I haven't spoken of this before now because I thought you had Steve and you were leaving at the end of the summer."

"Uh . . . okay."

His eyes dripped emotion. That same intense adoration I would see flashing from time to time.

"When you came to me last night and said you had broken up with Steve, the reason I froze and reacted as I did was because of this—" He waved his hand back and forth, indicating the space between us. "In order to move forward with our relationship, I knew then that I would have to tell you."

Move forward with our relationship? I liked the sound of that.

"Tell me what?" I asked.

"How my family came to be called the Damned Earls."

10

I froze. My brain struggled to follow his seemingly erratic logic.

"Let me get this straight. Your seizures are related to my Grandma's cookies and that connects to why you're a damned Earl?"

"More or less." He pulled his feet out of the water and turned sideways, leaning back against one of the arches. He propped his heels up on the wide, stone wall between us, head turned, staring over the view of rolling hills and valleys opposite the *fonti*.

Finally, he looked back to me. "I've actually never told this story to another person. It's not something we ever discuss outside of our immediate family—"

Whatever he intended to say was cut off.

Cesare jerked to stiff attention, his gaze instantly going unfocused.

Another absence seizure.

Panic choked me.

Was he terminally ill? Was this a hereditary thing? Did I need to run for medical help?

"Cesare?" I touched his leg. "Can you hear me? Should I get help?"

As usual with his seizures, he wasn't convulsing, nor did he appear to be in pain.

He was simply . . . immobile.

Helplessness washed over me. What was I supposed to do? Without knowing the cause of his odd episodes, it was hard to respond.

I simply had to wait.

I hopped down and walked forward in the water, pulling myself up to sit on the stone ledge facing him, my hips even with his thigh.

Up close, I realized his body trembled, like some charged force thrummed through it. His breaths came in short gasps, air rasping in his lungs.

I slipped an arm around his waist, burying my head into his shoulder. At least, if he collapsed, I could prevent him tumbling into the pool.

I fought my own panic. Was he dying, then? Epileptic? Brain tumor? It would explain why he was so sure he would bring me heartache. Half of me wondered what was wrong with him, the other half determined to help him through whatever it was.

After an eternity—but it was really only a few minutes—Cesare's shoulders slumped and his body came back to life, though the shaking didn't stop. He wrapped his arms tight around me, crushing my chest to his.

"Please, what's wrong?" I murmured in his ear. "I need to know, Cesare."

I pulled back from him, my eyes pleading with his. He kept a hand loose at my waist.

"I'm worried you won't believe me," he began.

"I will."

"That's why I made the cookies. I knew your logical, scientific mind would need proof."

Proof? Proof of what?

He swallowed. "Remember my ancestor I told you about earlier?"

"The one who made the family fortune here in San Gimignano?"

"The very same. Giovanni D'Angelo. There is a lot more to the family history regarding Giovanni."

"Like how he made his money?"

"Among other things. Family lore states that sometime in the late 1200s, Giovanni found himself outmaneuvered by competing families. He was losing ground fast and needed a solution. He found one."

Cesare let his head tilt back, resting against the stone arch, swallowing loudly, as if trying to work up the courage for something.

But . . . what? How could the actions of an ancestor nearly seven hundred years before matter to such a great extent today?

He sucked in a deep breath. "Giovanni visited the camp of some gypsies near here." He waved a hand outward, indicating the hills beyond the *fonti*. "And there, he essentially sold his soul—or more accurately, the souls of his descendants—in exchange for the gift of Second Sight."

My expression had grown frownier the longer Cesare spoke.

Second Sight? What did some old legend have to do with us and now?

His gaze cut back to mine, eyes still pleading for understanding.

Unfortunately, I wasn't sure I could give him any.

"So . . ." I blinked. "You're going to have to give me more here. I'm lost."

"Giovanni was granted a powerful gift of Second Sight—"

"What does that mean? Second Sight?"

He sighed. "In this case, it means the ability to see, hear and feel the past and the future. Giovanni used the knowledge he gained from his gift to outsmart his rivals, make brilliant investments, and so on. He quickly became fabulously wealthy and powerful."

My thoughts churned sluggishly. "But . . . what does this story have to do with you?"

Cesare said nothing. His eyes continued to bore into mine, expression plaintive.

I reared back slightly, realization jolting through me.

"No. You think—" I stopped, struggling to even get the words out. "You think *you* have this same gift? You have the ability to see the future and the past?"

Even saying the words out loud sounded crazy.

But Cesare obviously didn't think so.

"Precisely. The gift is hereditary."

"You have ESP . . . extrasensory perception?"

"Yes . . . of a sort."

"What does that mean? 'Of a sort'?"

"It means I see scenes of the past and possible visions of the future." He placed the words carefully, tentatively, as if I were a wild animal he expected to bolt.

I angled my head, staring at him.

Huh. He looked completely solemn.

But he *had* to be teasing. More of his challenging my tendency to be too logical. No way he was serious.

I laughed. "That's funny, Cesare. Be serious, though."

Silence.

His eyes continued to bore into mine. "I *am* serious, Judith. Deadly earnest."

"No way. You're pulling my leg. Ha-ha, funny joke. But for reals, how did you know about the cookies? Did you call my parents?"

More silence. More of his sincere staring, expression open and honest.

"I am telling the truth, Judith. I know you think that I'm joking, but I'm not. I do have the gift of Second Sight. If you look at it logically, such a gift explains all your concerns."

Fine. Mentally, I grudgingly acknowledged that such a talent would certainly explain things.

But—

No. No, I did not accept his explanation.

He was clearly delusional. He might believe he had some form of ESP, but such things did not exist.

There was a more commonplace, logical explanation.

"No." I shook my head again. "I don't—I can't—"

I tried to push away from him. Cesare held me firm. Not threatening, just insistent.

"Please listen to me, Judith. I know how you like your coffee because

I watched you prepare it in a vision. The same for the sandwich earlier—"

I paused, my palms on his chest. "You made that for me, too?"

"Of course. Italians don't normally put mustard on their *panini*. That's a German or French thing to do. As for the cookies, over and over, I've seen you making them with your grandma as a little girl."

Silence.

I didn't know what to say.

"I can't control the visions," he hastily clarified. "Not really. I can sometimes force them to come upon me, but I can't tell them specifically what I would like to see. I wasn't trying to pry into your past. But . . ." He shrugged again. "I adore you. You matter greatly to me. And because I tend to think about you a lot, many of my visions are about you."

Cesare adored me. Yay!

But—

"You see visions of me?"

Even coming out of my mouth, the words sounded silly. Visions? Really?

I was the scientist. *Just the facts, ma'am.*

I didn't do visions or paranormal or anything similar.

Poor Cesare. I knew he was too good to be true. No one could be so charming and kind and hunky.

"Like what kind of visions?" I asked. "Give me an example."

He didn't hesitate. "Meeting you."

"Me? You knew you would meet me?"

He smiled. "What? You think I perfected that cookie recipe in just the last day or two? I've been seeing you in my future for years now."

I froze again. "You've been seeing me for *years?*" My jaw hung open. "Th-that's . . . crazy."

"Perhaps. But as I said, the content of my visions is not something I can control. So though I have been seeing you for years, for some reason, I never heard your name. That's why I went to the piazza to meet you that day. I was desperate to know your name."

"You knew my grandma's cookie recipe but not my *name?*" I frowned. "How is that possible?"

Cesare shook his head ruefully. "Trust me, it was *incredibly* frustrating. I usually see big things before they happen. But it's not a precise science. For example, your arrival last night definitely surprised me. I hadn't seen it coming beforehand. And I definitely didn't know that you would break things off with Steve. Everything with Steve caught me off guard, to be honest. I've never seen Steve in any of my visions of you."

My brain struggled to catch up. He had known about me for *years*?!

I had about a hundred follow-up questions.

I started with, "So what other things have you seen about me?"

"All sorts of things. You were terribly cute as a child." A smile tugged at his lips. "You had this Holly Hobby obsession going, so you'd wear a . . . *pinafore* I think it's called. It was pink and blue patchwork with ruffles around the neck and at the hemline. The front had the words, *Work that's done in a cheerful way makes a busy fun-filled day* embroidered into it. I got the sense that your grandma had made it for you."

He continued to speak, my heart beating faster and faster with each word.

How did he know these things? I barely remembered them myself.

But he wasn't done.

"You made the cookies with your grandma in a small 1940s era kitchen that had white shaker cabinets and yellow flowered wallpaper. You would mix the cookies on a green vinyl table beside huge windows overlooking a large expanse of grass that stretched to a red barn out back. Your grandpa had farmed for a time, but the Dust Bowl of the 1930s bankrupted him, so he turned to ranching after World War II. I've wondered if your love of animals started on that farm. Your grandparents kept chickens, too. There was a mean rooster named Drumstick— your grandpa had funny names for all his animals—that used to cause you grief. I think he chased you up a tree once."

Drumstick had. I had never told anyone that story, not even my grandma. I had been ten at the time and too embarrassed to admit that a stupid rooster scared me that badly.

My hands trembled against Cesare's chest. My breathing tight and constricted.

Surely this was the beginning of a full-on panic attack.

How could Cesare possibly know all this? It was like he had cracked open my brain and extracted my deepest memories.

And still he talked. "Anyway, you would make cookies on that table with your grandma, and she'd tell you stories about her Scottish parents and look the other way when you'd snitch some of the cookie dough. When you placed the filled cookies on the cookie sheet, you couldn't put any in the right back corner because the oven burned in that place. Your grandma would always say you had to save the first cookie for your grandpa, but then she'd let you have the second. The hot filling would burn your mouth, but you didn't care. Nothing tasted as good as that cookie."

I was shaking so bad by the time he finished, I couldn't speak. I pulled my jittery hands off his chest and clasped them together.

It was all true. Every word.

Could my parents or siblings have told him all of this? Maybe.

But some of the details, like Drumstick, I didn't think anyone else would know. My grandparents were long gone, their old farm had been bulldozed ten years ago to make way for a new mall.

Cesare would have had to contact my mother. How would he have contacted them? Our phone number was unlisted. And even if he *had* tracked down my family, why would they tell him such specific details? Not to mention, how did he get Grandma's raisin cookie recipe so right? We all thought it had been lost.

Furthermore, why make up this crazy story about having Second Sight? What was there to gain from it?

Or was he just truly bonkers?

His eyes held pity.

"I know it's a lot to take in, Judith. And I don't expect you to believe me immediately. I know it will take time—"

"So that's what happens when you suddenly stop and stare off into space? It's not an absence seizure. You're having a vision?"

"Yeah."

"Is this why you're so sure you'll bring me heartache? Because you've seen it?" More silence. It stretched for too long.

"Cesare?"

He sighed and reached for my clasped hands, pulling one away and grasping it in his. My palms were cold and sweaty, the heat of his fingers burning me.

"I will tell you," he finally said, "but I can't promise that it won't freak you out."

More silence as I pondered this.

Now he worried about freaking me out?!

I was already at a pretty solid ten on the Freakout-O-Meter.

Did I really want to know what he saw?

Wait—

Was I actually considering this then? That Cesare had psychic abilities?

Logically, I didn't believe in ESP. But . . . what other explanation was there? The evidence in his favor was strong. Compelling, even.

Worse . . . I realized I *wanted* to believe him. I didn't want to think of Cesare as loony and psychotic and delusional.

Which . . . did that make *me* the delusional one?

Gah!

I would go insane with this logic merry-go-round.

A beat.

Finally, Cesare cleared his throat. "The gift grows in strength, year after year. Right now, it's strong and sometimes intrusive, but it's not debilitating. But as time goes on, I will start to hear and see and feel everything. And by that, I literally mean EVERYTHING. The noise will grow and grow until one day, it will fracture me from the inside out."

Oh. "And what happens then?"

A pause. And then his voice, low and firm:

"I die."

11

I flinched at his hard, unvarnished words. My head whipped back as if slapped, all the air punching from my lungs.

I stared at him, mouth flapping open, heart in my throat.

"I die," he repeated.

No.

I couldn't comprehend it.

No way this man was truly dying.

I bit my lip, trying to keep my emotions inside, desperate to stop the tears before I moved into the lip quivering stage.

"How? . . . You can't be *that* sure. It's just a p-possibility, right?"

Cesare continued to look at me, eyes kind and understanding, but haunted. So haunted.

He dragged a thumb across my cheek, staring at the moisture on it.

The tears I had been so diligently holding back overflowed.

Damn him. Now I *was* lip-quivering.

"I haven't seen my own death, Judith. But it's no accident that we're called the Damned Earls. The name is appropriate. I have read the records of the thirty-one D'Angelo men between Giovanni's time and mine. Every single one of them died, raving mad, at a young age. The vast majority by their own hand."

"Suicide?"

"Yes."

My mind short-circuited.

It was too much.

My tears quickly moved from lip-quivering to flat-out crying. Another minute and I would be in full hiccup-sobbing mode.

I slid off the ledge and stuffed my wet feet into my shoes, needing to put some distance between us.

I walked across the narrow lane, arms hugging my waist, and stared unseeing across the landscape. Smoke columns rose in the distance, farmers burning brush in a far-off field.

I sniffled and snuffled and hiccupped a time or two.

Cesare was a psychic.

He was slowly dying from his weird psychic-ness.

I focused on my breathing. In. Out.

It didn't help.

Neither of those facts computed with my logical understanding of reality.

I bit my lip and managed to swallow back some of my emotion.

I sensed more than saw Cesare join me.

"Your m-mother said your father had passed away. Was he p-part of this—" I swirled a finger, trying to find the right word. "—thing or gift or whatever?"

"I prefer the word *curse*, though I know Giovanni referred to it as a gift. And, yes, to answer your question. My father was completely insane by the end."

"How old were you?" For some reason, that seemed important to me.

"I was thirteen."

My stupid heart lurched.

So young.

My poor Cesare.

"D'Angelo heirs tend to die young. Most don't live past thirty-five. The curse gets to them. I've been doing better than previous generations—at least, I think I am. There are some anti-psychotic drugs that help dull the visions."

"How did he—" I broke off suddenly, not sure I wanted an answer.

"How did my father die?"

I nodded, biting my lip again.

"We're not entirely sure how it happened. You have to understand, Giovanni was the only D'Angelo to really want this 'gift.'" Cesare said *gift* with bitter irony. "The rest of us have spent our lives trying to get rid of it. Dad was convinced that water held the answer to solving the problem, something about needing to get away from people to smother it. Anyway, he took off in a yacht, aiming for open ocean. That was the last we ever heard from him. His empty boat was found bobbing weeks later. His body washed ashore a month after that."

Cesare said the words dispassionately, but a slight tremor betrayed the depth of his emotions.

"I'm so sorry," I said. I meant it.

I hazarded a glance at him. He was staring over the fields, eyes haunted and lost. A gentle breeze ruffled his dark hair.

He was *too* much.

My mind couldn't grapple with the thought of him being terminally ill. Surely he was mistaken.

"And you're convinced this will be your fate, too?"

"Yes." No doubt. "There is no escaping it, Judith. I feel it sometimes, hovering around the edges of my consciousness. It's a seething madness just waiting to push into me."

I looked away, back over the landscape.

"It's important for you to believe me, Judith. I want to be as open and honest with you as possible." He sighed. "So with that . . . there's one more thing you should know."

I couldn't look at him. Could my mind deal with any more of his *truths*?

He continued, "I refuse to pass along this curse to another generation. I refuse to have a son who will be fatherless at a young age. I refuse to continue to propagate my tainted bloodline." His voice was so determined, so firm. "The D'Angelos will die with me. I have taken steps to ensure I won't have children. Any woman I date needs to know this."

Silence hung for a moment.

"A vasectomy?" I had to ask.

"Yes."

I swallowed back the hysterical laughter that wanted to burst free.

Psychic, dying AND childless.

Man, did I know how to pick them or what?

Somewhere between the bland comfort of dating Steve and the wild, vivid *living* of being with Cesare, there had to be a middle ground.

But . . .

Though I hadn't known Cesare for long and I didn't know if I genuinely loved him, I did adore him. I certainly had an epic crush-to-end-all-crushes.

I wanted more than just a beautiful memory of him.

I genuinely wanted all his kisses.

And after finally experiencing the euphoric joy of being with him, how could I go back to less?

But how could I go forward?

The psychic thing baffled me.

The dying thing gutted me.

And children?

I honestly hadn't given children much serious thought. I loved my animals and working with them. I had wondered from time to time how a child would fit into all of it. At best, I was fairly ambivalent on the topic of kids. I was still young; there was time for that decision.

I finally turned to look at Cesare. His hazel eyes held so many emotions. Some I recognized—trepidation, hesitation, concern—and others I didn't.

An idea occurred to me. "One follow-up question. Are you opposed to children in general? Or just your own biological children?"

His reply was instant. "Just my own biological children. I love children in general. If I did marry and if my wife wanted children, we could pursue having a child some other way. There are solutions."

I nodded. Not ideal but workable.

So motherhood was still on the table for me.

"Look, Judith." Cesare gathered my hands in his again. "I know this is a lot to absorb. I just felt that you needed to know, partly because I don't like hiding things from you, but mostly so you can make informed decisions. I know how much you value logic and intellect."

"Cesare—"

"No, I meant that sincerely. I love your logical mind and careful reasoning. It's brilliant and charming and so very . . . *you*. And because I love those things about you, I want you to thoroughly understand the shape of the situation here."

I stared at our joined hands, my mind reeling and numb.

"Do you want me to leave?" I asked. "It feels like you're trying to drive me away."

"No. The selfish part of me desperately wants you to stay. I adore you, Judith Campbell. I loved you before I met you, and now, after meeting you, I can't imagine watching you walk away. I want more than just all your kisses. I want *all* your firsts from this point on."

"All my firsts?"

"Yes. Your first house, first gray hair, first major loss, first incredible employee success . . . everything."

Oh!

My heart flip-flopped, thrumming and burning. Abruptly, I was swallowing back tears again.

Cesare continued, "But I also care too much about you to allow you to feel trapped. If you choose to stay, I want it to be your own choice, free and clear."

"If I stay," I repeated. The idea instantly sank into me, burrowing deep.

I could choose to stay, couldn't I?

He nodded. "For the record, I still think you should run. You deserve so much more than my broken self."

I scoffed, shaking my head. "You're making assumptions about your health, Cesare. You don't *know* you're going to die. No one does—"

He cut me off. "I *can't* let you lie to yourself about this, Judith. I *will* die, sooner rather than later. You have to accept this—"

"No!" I dropped his hands, throwing them away from me. All of the emotion coursing through me coalesced into a burning ember of anger. "You don't get to tell me what to believe or think. You won't die! I won't let you!"

It suddenly seemed horrifically unfair that Cesare was dying. He couldn't die.

"You don't get to date me and make me adore you and tell me I'm beautiful and insist on all my kisses, just to up and die on me." I might have been shouting by this point, my finger jabbing him in the chest. "I won't let you die!"

"Can we go back to the part where you say you adore me?" He grinned. "I'd love to hear more about that."

"That's your takeaway here?! Ugh! Men!" I threw my hands into the air, stomping back to the *fonti*, intent on putting back on my socks.

"You adore me." Cesare's voice drifted behind me.

"Of *course* I adore you, and you know it. What with all your sweetness and kindness and hunkiness—"

"You think I'm hunky?"

I finished stuffing my feet back into my socks and retied my shoes.

I may have given him a serious stink-eye at that point. "Don't go changing the subject on me, Cesare. I'm serious. Half of me is tempted to stay here just to ensure you don't die."

"*Cara*—"

"Don't you *cara* me!" I came right back at him, my toes inches from his, my finger against his chest. "I'm not done with this conversation."

"*Dolcezza*, then?"

"Cesare—"

"Judith."

He took advantage of my closeness and wrapped his arms around my waist, pulling me against him and effectively scattering all logical thoughts from my brain.

"That's my favorite word, by the way," he continued. "Judith."

This man.

He made it impossible to stay upset with him.

He pressed his cheek to mine, nuzzling my throat, murmuring my name over and over.

"Judith. Sweet, sweet Judith. *Carissima. Bellissima.*"

I wanted more.

I turned my head toward him, seeking his mouth.

Cesare did not turn away.

I expected him to kiss me hungrily, eager and perhaps a bit sloppy.

But instead, he paused. Pulling back, he cupped my face and let every ounce of his adoration shine through his eyes.

Cesare bent his head down. My eyes fluttered shut.

He pressed his lips into mine.

Soft, gentle, coaxing. Worshipful.

Infinitely tender. As if I was a treat he intended to slowly savor.

His kiss was an explosion of sensation. Color burst behind my eyelids, a kaleidoscope of reds and blues and yellows.

I think he intended to kiss me and then pull back.

But I was having none of that.

I moaned into his mouth, arching into him.

He was not slow on the uptake.

Our kisses rapidly escalated.

Desperation washed me.

Cesare could not be dying.

I hadn't found this incredible human being just to lose him again.

There had to be some other explanation.

But what if there's not? A small part of me whispered. *What if he truly is psychic and dying?*

And if so, what will you do?

I cast the thought away.

I wasn't ready for big questions.

In the moment, I simply wanted all the kisses Cesare had promised me.

The next two weeks were a haze of delirious happiness and horrific confusion.

Cesare was the delirious happiness. We were officially dating, boyfriend and girlfriend, spending every available minute together.

The confusion, of course, came from thinking about his 'gift' and the fact that he was dying.

Worse, I only had three short weeks before boarding a plane back to Portland and my life there. What was I going to do?

Did I truly believe Cesare's tale of ancient curses and Second Sight? The scientist in me was equal parts fascinated and disbelieving.

I had, of course, cornered my mom and sisters and asked if they had spoken with him about Grandma and my past, but they were honestly baffled.

Cesare—like the patient, humble man that he was—didn't pressure me to make a decision or to completely commit to believing he had psychic abilities.

If he were delusional or trying to emotionally manipulate me, he wouldn't tell me he was a psychic and then let the facts speak for themselves.

Instead, he was behaving exactly the way a scientist would expect him to behave if he were telling the truth. I was pretty sure he was doing that to ease my logical mind into his reality.

And his methodology worked.

Slowly, I came to believe that Cesare's abilities were real.

Or rather, my brain caught up to what my heart had already told me was true.

He would simply know things before they happened, or would tell me about a vision of my past that no one else knew.

He told me about the vision he had of the little boy falling into the River Arno and then seeing himself rescuing the child.

The data points were staggering and overwhelming. If Cesare wasn't psychic, what other explanation was there?

During those two weeks, I would ask him questions about us and his curse. He would patiently answer.

Cesare would also offer up ideas of his own.

For example, a few days after our chat in San Gimignano, Cesare turned to me as we walked home one evening, hand-in-hand. The night sky was dark and soft rain misted the sidewalk.

"I found out something I wanted to let you know," he said.

"What?"

"I know you have a job waiting for you back in Portland at the end of the summer, but I spoke with some contacts who run a veterinary hospital just outside of downtown Florence. They're short staffed and would really like an English-speaking veterinarian to help with all the international customers they have. I could easily speak with the right people to get you an Italian work visa. It would mean staying here and learning Italian in earnest, but . . . just wanted you to see that there is a place for you here, a way for you to continue doing what you love." He squeezed my fingers.

Whoa.

I processed that information, sorting through all my emotions about it.

"What if—" I began, still thinking. "What if I don't want to give up my job in Portland? What if I want you to come with *me*?"

That threw him. Cesare paused, pulling me to a stop, expression surprised.

"Who says we both have to stay here?" I continued. "What if I kept my job in Portland and you came back to the States with me? You could move your business headquarters overseas."

He shook his head. "I haven't seen any visions of that."

Now it was my turn to look confused. "Do you always see visions of things you'll do?"

"No, there is a lot I don't see. Having a gift of foresight is not the same as being omniscient. I know only the small slices my gift chooses to show me."

"Well, you think about it, too," I countered.

"I will."

We walked on in silence for a moment longer.

"It's mostly my mother I worry about," he finally said. "I'm all she has. But she could visit often."

Of course, his concern for his mother melted my heart. I was coming to love her. I had made pasta with Alice more than once and laughed with her, each of us trying to understand the other despite the language barrier.

In addition to asking and answering questions, Cesare showed me more of his favorite places in Tuscany, including the spectacular family villa—named Villa Maledetti, of course—nestled in the rolling hills outside Volterra.

The old place had been shuttered up for a number of years—not enough family members to keep it open regularly—but Cesare liked escaping there. I was coming to realize that he found it difficult sometimes to be around a lot of people. The added cacophony of visions they brought made his life that much more difficult. So he would retreat to Villa Maledetti from time to time, when the 'noise' got to be too much, he would say.

Additionally, I struggled to understand his complete acceptance of his fate. He never wavered from his insistence that he would die young, that if I stayed with him, I would watch him go mad.

I started to feel as if we were tethered together. I was the hawk, soaring high and free and Cesare was my falconer. He let me fly as high as I wished, but a bond tied us together, and without that bond, I worried I would float away and never find myself grounded again.

Or perhaps the opposite, without his encouraging hand, I would tumble to the ground and never get up, cursed to live my life without Cesare's euphoric highs and lows.

Obviously, abstract, metaphorical thinking was not my forte.

I missed Cesare desperately when we were apart. My emotions lifted when we were together.

But was that love? Did I love him?

I found myself becoming emotional over the stupidest things. Crying over a pigeon, hurt and bleeding, limping down the sidewalk. Or Cesare bringing me flowers. Or a baby diaper commercial.

When I thought about leaving Cesare in September . . . yeah, that was serious ugly-crying.

But how would we work? Could he handle living in Portland with me? I wasn't sure I was ready to cut all ties with my former life and remain in Florence with him.

I was officially pathetic.

I felt frozen. Panicked. Unable to move forward or back.

Logic was failing me here and I didn't know where to turn.

How could I make this impossible decision?

BY THE LAST WEEK OF August, I felt like I was rushing head-long toward the edge of a cliff.

All signs screaming, 'Disaster Ahead!'

I had to make a decision, or the decision would be made for me.

I had a return airplane ticket. I had a job and an apartment waiting for me.

No decision was still a decision.

But I also struggled to find the sign that said, *Yes, stay*.

Eight days before my flight home, I was getting ready for bed when panicked thoughts hit with brutal force.

What if I never saw him again?

What if he died before I could say goodbye?

What if I stayed with him and had to watch him die?

Would I be okay never having children?

What if we *had* children and I became Alice, watching my own boy struggle with this debilitating 'ability'?

Cesare refused to help me make the decision. He said it needed to be mine.

I couldn't talk to my mom or sisters or friends about it. They wouldn't be able to get past the 'by the way, he's a terminally ill psychic' part. Ditto with Kimberly or Sandra. They knew something was up, but they just assumed it was the angst of knowing my time with Cesare had a definite end date.

Hah!

They were right, just not like they assumed.

So . . . it was just me. My own thoughts. And what I wanted my life to be.

Did I belong here? Could I remain?

Could Cesare follow me home?

The logical, conservative decision would be to kiss Cesare goodbye, store away my beautiful memories and return to my predictable life in Portland.

That thought made me feel ill.

But how could I accept the messy, unknown opposite of that?

I kept thinking about Kimberly's words in Paris, that when you love someone, you just know.

Did I love Cesare? Sometimes, I thought, yes, maybe I did. I could see us together, being a couple, committed to each other. But then I would think about the uncertainty of a life with him and panic would grip my chest and then I wasn't sure anymore.

And even if I did love him, I knew that sometimes love just wasn't enough. If what Cesare believed was true, would I still choose to love him, even knowing the heartache waiting at the end for me?

That was the question I couldn't answer. The final leap of faith I wasn't sure I was ready to make.

But giving up Cesare felt equally impossible.

And so I floated through the days simply existing.

I WAS SITTING IN MY bedroom alone one early evening only five days before I was supposed to go home. Sunset washed my room in reds and golds, sending long purple shadows sprawling up the walls.

Kimberly and Sandra weren't home, choosing to spend their last few days in Vienna (Kimberly had four more lips to kiss, and Sandra wanted to research coffee habits in Austria). Cesare was busy, having pressing work problems to deal with.

So that left me with my thoughts. Never a good thing. I was sorting through postcards on my bed, reliving events of the past few months. The collected images were memory time capsules—San Gimignano, Paris, San Marco, Uffizi, Galileo, Rome.

A postcard of *Judith Slaying Holofernes* tumbled out of the stack, dropping to my pillow.

Huh.

The postcard Cesare had purchased for me that first day in the Uffizi. Judith, fierce and determined, beheading the Assyrian general. But also Artemisia, fierce and determined, metaphorically cutting her rapist from her life.

What had driven Artemisia to continue to fight—

Bzzz. Bzzz.

The front doorbell buzzed, causing me to jump.

I raced to the door, postcard in hand. Cesare must have finished early.

Instead, it was Alice who smiled at me from atop the doormat.

She turned a letter over and over in her hands.

"Ciao." She greeted me.

"Ciao."

She huffed and then rattled something off in Italian that I couldn't understand.

I smiled and shrugged.

She shook her head. "I sorry I no speak English."

"That's okay. I don't speak Italian either." Though I had been learning. "*Io non parlo italiano molto bene.*"

I don't speak Italian very well.

She nodded and handed me the letter she had in her hand.

"For you." She cocked her head, thinking. "I use *dizionario*—"

"Dictionary?"

"*Sì* and a friend—" She mimed writing with a pen. "—*mi ha aiutato.*"

Oh! "You wrote me a letter that a friend and the dictionary helped you translate."

Alice smiled brightly. "*Sì.*"

She hesitated and then bopped up on her tiptoes, kissing me on the cheek, the motion feeling so natural and normal, my eyes instantly stung.

How could I leave Alice, too?

"*Ti volgio un saccone di bene, cara,*" she murmured.

I knew that much Italian—*I love you so much.* But 'I love you' in a non-amorous sort of way. What you said between friends—literally, *I want a sack of good for you.*

"*Grazie mille,*" I whispered through my tears. "*Ti voglio bene anch'io.*"

I traded her cheek kiss for a very American hug, engulfing her in my arms. To her credit, she squeezed me back.

"*Buona serata.*" She patted my arm and pointed at the letter. And then left, heels clicking down the stairs.

13

After Alice left, I stared at her letter in one hand, the postcard of Artemisia's *Judith* in the other.

It seemed fitting to be holding them both.

I closed the door on my quiet apartment and took the final flight of stairs, letting myself out onto the rooftop of the D'Angelo's palazzo.

The last rays of sunlight kissed the horizon, razing the city in shapes of light and dark against the hills beyond.

I had been up here before but had found the rooftop a neglected space. Just a flat expanse of porcelain tiles. It needed a dining table and loggia with potted plants, maybe a pretty railing around the edge. Something.

I crossed the terrace and slipped around a built-up half wall, intent on the gorgeous views on the other side. The vista was spectacular, taking in the tiled rooftops of Florence, the Duomo standing tall above them. I slid down the wall, sitting on the still-warm flagstones, staring out over the city.

Curious, I carefully opened Alice's envelope and pulled out a sheet of paper, lined with handwriting. Tilting the paper into the remaining sunlight, I read the scrawling English.

My dearest Giudetta . . . the letter began.

Giudetta. Judith.

I could hear Alice saying my name in Italian—joo-DEH-tah.

I smiled and continued reading.

> *I hope you will forgive the presumption of this letter. I know we haven't known each other long, but my heart already understands that you are a part of it. I have enjoyed your company this summer. In particular, I have loved watching you bring light to my Cesare's life. Carrying the burden of the D'Angelo curse is not easy. I know this better than anyone else alive.*

> *When I learned the truth about my Alessio, Cesare's father, I cried for two weeks straight. I already loved him by that point and couldn't imagine a world without him. I realized I faced a simple choice: stay or go?*

> *After another day of crying, I decided to stay. He was too wonderful and I was too in love. I would mourn him regardless of when we parted. Why not have a few blissful years with him before . . . well, you know?*

My throat closed off, raw and aching, something thick caught in it. Her words lingered, resonating deeply.

I would mourn him regardless of when we parted. Why not have a few blissful years?

Wasn't that the truth?

I continued on.

> *In the end, I got more than just a few years, nearly fifteen to be exact. I cared for Alessio through it all. Bit by bit, I watched the madness consume him until the man I adored more than life itself ceased to exist. It was a pain unlike any other, to lose him like that, piece after tiny piece.*

Something wet hit my hand. I wiped my cheeks.

It is not easy to love a D'Angelo man. For me, having Alessio's love and care for the years that I did were worth the price of losing him. I do not regret any portion of my life with him.

I imagine you find yourself at a similar crossroads. I see how you look at my Cesare when his eyes are elsewhere. He is your sun and your moon, the very light of your world—just as his father was the light of mine. I would never trade even a minute of my life for anyone else's, pain and all. I have had the love of two extraordinary men—my Alessio and my Cesare—and my heart is full because of it.

I know your choice is not a simple one, my child. I wish I could say that the path forward would be easy with Cesare. It will not be. It will be the highest highs paired with the lowest of lows. But ask yourself, if you left him now, would your pain be any less?

I was sobbing in earnest now. Trust Alice to find a way to express everything that was already in my heart.

Regardless of the outcome, I would mourn Cesare. I could mourn him now and move on, or I could have a few precious years with him . . . before the end.

But Alice wasn't done. I read the last bit of text.

We often seek to control our lives. We want the way laid out for us with ruthless precision, clearly showing us the path, one logical step at a time. A color-coded map. But I've come to realize that isn't how living works. Life isn't a journey along a defined path.

Life is a crazy vacation. No map. A constant sense of shifting destination. Unexpected stops and false starts. In life, the journey is almost irrelevant. You won't end where you thought you would. No one does. But you can choose who you share the journey with. Who will be your travel companion? I chose Alessio D'Angelo, and I have never regretted it.

Regardless of what you choose, know that I genuinely love you and consider you my daughter in every way that matters.

   With all my love,

   Alice

I pulled my knees up to my chest and sobbed. Heaving, gut-wrenching, hiccupping, my-heart-is-breaking sobs.

Life isn't a journey along a defined path.

Who will be your travel companion?

Like that moment in Paris with Kimberly, it all hit me with stark clarity.

I prided myself on my level head, on logic, on my clear course into the future.

But . . . that wasn't life. Not true capital-L *Living.*

I wiped my eyes with my free palm and, in the process, glanced at the postcard of Artemisia's *Judith* still in my hand.

I instantly choked up again.

Here was the painting of a woman who chose the messier path. It would have been easier to remain quiet, to not fight back. But I instinctively understood that Artemisia had loved herself and her art too much to be silent.

Artemisia Gentileschi was a woman willing to fight her demons. Quite literally in her case.

I would fight demons for Cesare.

And again like that day along the Seine, suddenly . . . I knew.

I loved Cesare D'Angelo.

All my emotions for him—adoration, respect, admiration, attraction, devotion—spun around and around each other, drawing tighter and tighter together until they simply collapsed into one bright, shiny, crystalline emotion:

I loved him.

I loved Cesare D'Angelo.

Utterly. Completely. Irrevocably.

It flooded me—aching awareness. Giddy devotion mixed with blinding happiness and a giant helping of frozen terror.

I chose it. I welcomed it.

My love for him had probably been there for weeks already, simply waiting for me to push aside my fear and embrace the illogic of it.

I hiccupped and snuffled and eventually had to use my t-shirt to dry my eyes.

I raised my head. And gasped.

Cesare stood in front of me. In the noise of my sobs, I hadn't heard the door open or his footsteps.

He stood ten feet away, hands in his pockets, face mournful. He was shadow and form in the dim light—one side of his body lit by the fading sunset, the rest of him dark and undefined.

And didn't that sum up Cesare as a whole? Parts of him fascinatingly lit up, bright and shining. But there were depths there that I didn't understand and probably never would.

Chiaroscuro.

"You can still walk away." His voice deepened, rough with emotion. "You can still let me be a beautiful memory."

I shook my head.

My love for him flared. Supernova bright. A burst of emotion so intense it nearly blacked my vision.

"No—" I hiccupped. Stopped. Drew in a stuttering breath and tried again.

I pushed to my feet, shoulders pressing against the wall to hold myself upright.

"No," I repeated more strongly now. "I d-don't want a beautiful memory."

He froze. Eyes wide and wary.

I stalked toward him, finger jabbing his way as I spoke. "I'm a memory hoarder, Cesare. I'm stingy and selfish."

He watched me come, unmoving, resigned to whatever fate I doled out. I stopped in front of him, gazing searchingly.

"I don't want a single, beautiful memory—" I choked, my throat aching. I licked tears off my upper lip.

"I want *all* your memories, my love," I whispered. "Every. Last. One."

His chest collapsed. His eyes closed. Pain, agony, despair, joy, elation . . . each flitted across his face.

He mouthed the words back to me. *My love.*

I waited for him to reopen his eyes. The shimmer in his matched the shimmer in my own.

"I want *all* your m-memories," I hiccupped. "I want every memory you have from now 'til the day you d-die—"

He crushed me to him, stealing my words with his lips.

I poured myself into our kiss. Hopes. Dreams.

"I love you, Cesare D'Angelo," I whispered against his mouth.

It seemed imperative that I say those precise words. They had been stuck in my throat for too long.

A huge gust of air left him, as if he had been holding his breath since we met and only now allowed himself to breathe properly.

"I love you," I repeated, "and I don't want us to be apart."

He was crying now, holding me to him, enormous gasps racking his large body. I tried to pull back, to kiss him more, but he refused to let me. As if his emotion embarrassed him, and he wanted to pretend it didn't exist.

I knew something about that.

We both cried for a good long while. For me, it was releasing all the emotion I had been holding inside for weeks now.

The pain that loving Cesare would inevitably bring me.

The sorrow over his life being cut short.

The sheer relief of having made a decision and knowing I had forever altered the course of my life.

Finally acknowledging to myself that some things were logically unknowable, and yet I emotionally *felt* the truth of them bone deep—

I loved Cesare D'Angelo.

And I was going to act on those feelings.

Eventually, his mouth found mine again, claiming my lips as his own. He tasted of possibility and home.

He pressed his forehead to mine.

"I love you, too, *carissima mia.*" He stopped, convulsively swallowing before he could continue. "I've loved you for longer than I can remember. I loved you before I met you, and I'll love you 'til my last breath. You and only ever you."

We kissed on and on, until the night purpled and the lights turned golden in the dark.

Eventually, I pulled back from him. He grasped my chin, coaxing me to look at him. I did with a wobbly smile.

"So . . . now what?" I murmured.

"Aside from me having all your kisses and you having all my memories?" he teased.

I chuckled, watery and sniffly.

He thumbed my cheek. "I had a vision earlier today."

"Really?"

He nodded. "It's one I've been having over and over."

"What is it? Why haven't you talked about it?"

"I didn't want to freak you out."

"Ah. It's a freak-out vision. So why tell me now?"

"I'm not sure you'll find it so freaky anymore." He kissed my forehead. "I keep seeing our wedding day. I see you walking down the aisle to me in a gorgeous white gown. I see us saying our vows to each other. I see you cutting our wedding cake with me. I see you at my side, flash bulbs firing, as the wedding photographer tells me to kiss you again."

Oh.

Wow.

Yes.

Please.

That.

I wanted that moment with a visceral ache.

Us. Together.

Tears flooded me again. How I still had any to shed, I had no idea.

"Yes, p-please," I hiccupped. "Let's do that."

"You're going to be stuck with me now," he laughed. "Beautiful Judith . . . I don't think I can ever thank you enough."

"Thank me?"

"For being the Golden Girl willing to join me in the dark. My saving angel."

"No. I'm not joining you in the dark. That's not how this works. I'm no one's salvation."

"You're not?"

"Nope. You already live in the light. I'm just here insisting you recognize the light. That's the only thing *golden* about me."

He pecked my lips. "Thank you for showing me the light."

"*Di niente,*" I replied, literally *of nothing*, but meaning, 'you're welcome.'

As I kissed Cesare on the rooftop that night, I knew nothing of the heartache ahead.

I suspected. But that's not the same as *knowing*.

Yet all that future heartache came with great joy.

I will be forever grateful to have had *all* of Cesare D'Angelo's memories.

I could only echo what Alice said:

We can't know the highs without knowing the lows. Though unexpected and full of loss and pain, I wouldn't trade a minute of my life with Cesare.

I will always choose harder, messier chaos over logical sameness.

Illogical though it may be, love cannot be measured or rationally explained.

It just is.

And, despite knowing the end from the beginning, I would never regret loving Cesare D'Angelo.

EPILOGUE

His vision happened just as he had seen: Judith walking down the aisle toward him, impossibly beautiful in her billowy white gown.

Once she had decided to be with him, there had been no looking back. Not for her. But that was Judith—loyal, committed, fierce in her love.

Cesare could scarcely believe that this beautiful, intelligent, amazing woman had chosen him.

Though Judith had been willing to remain with him in Florence, he wanted her to have the career she had spent years working toward in Portland. He would return to Italy often to visit Alice. So Cesare left with Judith in September.

Oregon flooded his visions of the future: him roaming the forest of the Pacific Northwest, getting a coffee in downtown Portland with Judith laughing at his side, the two of them cozy in a small rented farmhouse just outside town. Judith waking in the morning, hair mussed, face sleepy and looking so impossibly beautiful, he felt as if his heart would burst.

He hated that he couldn't see all of his future, not in its entirety.

He could sense the madness hovering at his edges, waiting to snatch him up. But *when* that would happen, he didn't know. Like his father, he would probably lose himself, piece by piece, until there wasn't enough of him to continue living.

But he didn't know the time frame of that.

Everything beyond a certain point was blank, as if his 'gift' was waiting for something to happen and the future hung in the balance.

Was it his death? Judith's? The end of the world?

It all became clear to him one day about eight months after their marriage.

He lurched awake, the sound of a resounding *crack* still lingering in his memory. It had been a fracturing sound, glass smashing or ice shattering.

Heart racing, adrenaline pumping, he sat up in bed, listening, assessing.

Judith turned over, sleepily looking up at him.

"What's wrong?" she murmured.

"I don't know. Did you hear anything?"

"Nohm," she mumbled, slipping back into sleep.

Unable to sleep, he stumbled out of bed, checking all the windows and locks in the house, even going so far as to fetch a flashlight and scour the backyard, too.

Nothing.

Nothing broken or amiss.

What had happened? He had definitely heard something.

He sat on the couch, concentrating.

That's when he realized. He felt . . . different.

Like something had changed, some force within him shifting or morphing and then realigning itself.

What the—?

It was odd.

But that sense of *something* having altered remained.

He didn't say anything about it to Judith. She was working hard in her new veterinarian position, and she already worried enough over him. Why add another thing to her load?

Six weeks later, he had his answer.

Judith came home from work early, stumbling through the door and racing for the bathroom where she was violently sick.

He held her hair back as she heaved over the toilet.

"I'm so sorry," she whispered. "All the smells at work just hit me at once, ya know. I kept gagging until they said I just needed to go home and get feeling better. I'm sure I'll be fine by tomorrow."

But she wasn't fine.

By the third day, Cesare started to have some suspicions.

A trip to Walgreen's and a pregnancy test confirmed what he already suspected:

Judith was pregnant.

Against all the odds, the unthinkable had happened.

He was going to be a father.

A larger shock came months later when an ultrasound revealed she was carrying not one baby, but three.

Triplets.

Their conception had changed something with the D'Angelo curse. He sensed it. The change wouldn't come in time for him. He would still suffer and go the same route as his father and grandfather and so on back into history.

But . . . as he walked down the hospital corridor to visit his three tiny boys in their bassinets for the first time, he thought that perhaps, for them, things might be different. Only hours old and he already loved his boys—Dante, Branwell and Tennyson—with passionate intensity.

He stood outside the glass, looking into the nursery, feeling equal parts elation and terror at the thought of being responsible for those three little beings.

Raising his camera, he snapped a photo of them together. He whispered a prayer to whatever being would listen to please save his boys. Give them freedom from the curse that damned him and every other D'Angelo male for the past seven hundred years.

Something. Anything.

Just please . . . give them a future.

Later that same day, he tenderly kissed Judith's forehead as she lay in the hospital bed, exhausted but blissfully happy, tiny Dante tucked into one arm, Branwell in the other. Cesare held Tennyson.

She looked up at him. "Thank you," she whispered.

"Thank me?" He chuckled. "No, *cara*, you are the goddess here, not me. Thank you for my wonderful boys. They're beautiful."

How he loved this woman.

"Can I ask you a question?" She smiled, that broad, lush smile he would never tire of seeing.

"Of course, my love."

"We just had three of these little guys, so I assume we're going to be insanely busy for a while. But—" She paused and bounced Dante in her right arm. "—the damage is sorta done. The curse only attaches to the first-born son, so I was thinking, maybe in a couple years . . ."

He grinned, shaking his head. "Are you saying you'd like more children, *cara*?"

"You have to admit a daughter would be nice."

"Someone for the boys to torture?"

"Are you sure that's how it would go down? Maybe *she* would torment them?" Wry humor lit Judith's face.

He laughed aloud at that. It instantly punched through him, the vision of a dark-haired, dark-eyed little girl, hands on her hips, bossing her older three brothers around.

Love for her choked him.

"Yes, *cara mia*, I would love to have a daughter. But let's give these three boys a chance to grow a bit first."

Judith smiled and closed her eyes, clearly exhausted. He thought she had fallen asleep, but after a few minutes she spoke.

"I know there will be heartache for us yet." Her voice barely louder than a whisper. "But you have brought me such unimaginable happiness."

"*Cara*—"

"No, please don't wave away my words, darling." She opened her eyes, love and adoration shining in their blue depths. "I want you to know that, even if I had a hundred lifetimes, I would choose the uncertain chaos of our life together over any other. It's not logical, but as a wise man I know once insisted, logic and feeling aren't in opposition to each other, but simply two different tools we use to arrive at truths."

He swallowed, emotion clogging his throat.

"I love you, Cesare D'Angelo," she whispered. "Thank you for believing in me. Thank you for being my partner in all this." She lifted the babies in her arms.

"I love you, too, *cara*." He bent and kissed her softly.

"Thank you for being my most true truth," she murmured against his lips. "For being my deepest, most illogical feeling."

"No," he returned, "thank you, Golden Girl, for being my everything. All my alls."

AUTHOR'S NOTE

*L*overs and Madmen is the story I never intended to publish.

I had written parts of Judith and Cesare's love story as backstory and brainstorming for the entire Brothers Maledetti series. It helped to have the timing of events firmly laid out in my series bible so I didn't run into continuity errors.

But as I wrote *Lightning Struck* and *A Madness Most Discreet*, my mind kept turning again and again to Judith and Cesare and their story until I just knew—I had to turn my notes and scenes into something more complete.

Initially, I thought it would simply be a short story, just that first scene of them meeting. But that scene led to another and another and before long the book was a novella . . . and then I revised it and it went from novella to near full-novel length.

I've loved delving into my memories of Italy and Europe in the 1980s, though I was first there a few years later than 1982. That said, Europe as a tourist was drastically different before the Iron Curtain fell, before cell phones and the Internet.

A few notes:

Every place mentioned in the book is one you can visit: the Galileo museum, the Uffizi, the Museum of San Marco with its frescoes and tiny monk cells. In particular, the town of San Gimignano with its *fonti mediovali* is one of my favorite places on Planet Earth. Returning there always feels like pilgrimage.

Artemisia Gentileschi was absolutely a real-life person whose life I have tried to accurately represent in the story. The only liberty I took was placing several of her paintings in the Uffizi, when some are in the Palazzo Pitti across the Arno from the Uffizi Gallery. (At least, that's where they are located today. I honestly have no idea where both paintings were housed in 1982.) Regardless, Gentileschi was an absolutely fascinating human being who spent her life fighting for a place as a woman in a man's world.

I have created an extensive pinboard on Pinterest with images of everything I talk about in the book. There was quite a bit to pin of all the locations and paintings, so if you want a visual of anything, pop over there and explore. Just search for NicholeVan.

As with all books, this one couldn't have been written without the help and support from those around me. I know I am going to leave someone out with all these thanks. So to that person, know that I totally love you and am so deeply grateful for your help!

To my beta readers—you know who you are—thank you for your helpful ideas and support. And, again, an extra-large thank you to Erin Rodabough, Annette Evans and Norma Melzer for their fantastic editing skills and insights.

For all her editorial help and insights, Rebecca Spencer deserves accolades and laurel wreaths, or barring that, a lengthy spa-day and endless Cadbury chocolate. Her assistance and refusal to accept my mediocre first efforts spurred me to make the story sparkle more. Bec, thanks for reminiscing about Europe in the 1980s and swapping long stories about kissing European men and traveling when all we had was a Eurail timetable, traveler's cheques, *Frommers,* and lots of optimism.

And, finally, thank you to Andrew, Austenne, Kian and Dave for putting up with my endless questions and not being too judgy of my somewhat out-of-control relationship with energy drinks. I love you.

OTHER BOOKS BY NICHOLE VAN

BROTHERHOOD OF THE BLACK TARTAN

Suffering the Scot
Romancing the Rake
Loving a Lady
Making the Marquess
Remembering Jamie (Autumn 2021)

OTHER REGENCY ROMANCES

Seeing Miss Heartstone
Vingt-et-Un | Twenty-one (a novella included in *Falling for a Duke.*)
A Ring of Gold (a novella included in *A Note of Change.*)

BROTHERS *MALEDETTI*

Lovers and Madmen
Gladly Beyond
Love's Shadow
Lightning Struck
A Madness Most Discreet

THE HOUSE OF OAK

Intertwine
Divine
Clandestine
Refine
Outshine

If you haven't yet read *Seeing Miss Heartstone*,
please turn the page for a preview of this
Whitney Award Winner for Best Historical Romance 2018.

SEEING MISS HEARTSTONE

. . . My lord, news of your current financial pressures has reached many ears. I know of an interested party who would be honored to discuss a proposed joint venture. They have asked to meet you along the Long Water in Hyde Park tomorrow morning, where they shall endeavor to lay out the particulars of their proposal . . .

—excerpt from an unsigned letter posted to Lord Blake

In retrospect, Miss Arabella Heartstone had three regrets about 'The Incident.'

She should not have worn her green, wool cloak with the fox fur collar, as Hyde Park was warmer than expected that morning.

She should not have instructed her chaperone, Miss Anne Rutger, to remain politely out of earshot.

And she probably should *not* have proposed marriage to the Marquess of Blake.

"P-pardon?" Lord Blake lifted a quizzical eyebrow, standing straight and tall, rimmed in the morning sunlight bouncing off the Long Water behind him. A gentle breeze wound through the surrounding trees, rustling newly-grown, green leaves. "Would . . . would you mind repeating that last phrase? I fear I did not hear you correctly."

Belle straightened her shoulders, clasped her trembling hands together, and sternly ordered her thumping heart to *Cease this racket.*

Swallowing, she restated her request. "After much consideration, my lord, I feel a marriage between you and myself would be prudent."

Lord Blake stared at her, blinking over and over. Belle was unsure if his reaction denoted surprise or was simply the result of the dazzling sunlight off the water behind her.

Silence.

Birds twittered. Branches creaked. Leaves rustled.

Eternities passed. Millennia ended and were reborn.

Belle gritted her teeth, desperate to bolster her flagging confidence. *You are strong and courageous. You can do this.*

In the past, her passivity over the Marriage Matter had nearly ended in disaster. So, Belle had set her sights on a more forthright course—propose marriage herself. Yes, she struggled to talk with people and preferred anonymity to attention, but her current situation was critical.

She needed a husband. Decidedly. Desperately. Immediately. As in . . . yesterday would not have been soon enough.

At the moment, however, her mental encouragement barely managed to convince the swarming butterflies in her stomach to not free her breakfast along with themselves. Casting up her accounts all over his lordship's dusty Hessian boots would hardly nurture his romantic interest.

At last, Lord Blake stirred, pulling a folded letter from his overcoat. He stared at it, eyebrows drawing down, a sharp "V" appearing above his nose.

"You sent me this message, asking to meet me here?" He flapped the letter in her direction.

"Yes." Belle bit down on her lip and darted a glance behind at her companion. Miss Rutger stood a solid thirty yards off, studiously facing the Long Water. "Well . . . uhm . . . in all truthfulness, Miss Rutger wrote the letter."

Lord Blake raised his eyebrows, clearly uncaring of the minutiae involved. "So you are *not* a gentleman interested in my business venture in the East Indies?" He unfolded the letter, reading from it. "'*I know of an interested party who would be honored to discuss a proposed joint venture. They have asked to meet you along the Long Water*,' et cetera. This 'interested party' is yourself?" He returned the letter to his pocket.

"Yes, my lord." Belle commanded her feet to hold still and not bounce up and down—the bouncing being yet another effect of those dratted nervous butterflies.

Lord Blake's brows rose further. "And you are offering . . . marriage?"

"Yes, my lord," Belle repeated, but she had to clarify the point. Apparently, she had no issue with being thought forward and brazen, but heaven forbid Lord Blake imagine her a liar, too. "Though . . . I *am* proposing a joint endeavor."

"Indeed," he paused. "Marriage usually implies as much."

Lord Blake shuffled a Hessian-booted foot and clasped his hands behind his back. A corner of his mouth twitched.

Was the man . . . amused? If so, was that good? Or bad?

And at this point, did it matter?

Belle soldiered on. "There would be significant advantages to both of us with such a match."

More silence. An errant draft of wind tugged at his coat.

"You have me at a disadvantage, Miss . . ." His voice trailed off.

"Heartstone. Miss Arabella Heartstone."

"I see." He removed his hat and slapped it against his thigh. "And why have we not met in more . . . uh . . . typical circumstances? A ball, perhaps? A dinner party where we could be properly introduced and engage in conversation about the weather and the latest bonnet fashions before leaping straight to marriage?"

"Oh." It was Belle's turn to blink, absorbing his words. *Oh dear.* "We *have* met, my lord. We were introduced at Lord Pemberley's musicale last month. We did discuss the weather, but not bonnets or . . . uhm . . . marriage."

She hadn't expected him to recall everything, but to not even *recognize* her? To not remember their brief conversation—

"*How do you do, Miss Heartstone? It's a pleasure to make your acquaintance.*" Lord Blake bowed.

"*The pleasure is all mine, my lord.*" Belle curtsied. "*Lovely weather we're having.*"

"*Indeed, we are.*"

It did not bode well.

The butterflies rushed upward, eager for escape.

"Right." Blake let out a gusting breath and shook his head, sending his hair tumbling across his forehead. The morning sun turned it into molten shades of deep amber, curling softly over his ears.

Lean and several inches taller than her own average height, Lord Blake was not classically handsome, she supposed. His straight nose, square jaw, and high forehead were all too exaggerated for classical handsomeness.

And yet, something about him tugged at her. Perhaps it was the breadth of his shoulders filling out his coat. Or maybe it was the ease of his stance, as if he would face the jaws of Hell itself with a sardonic smile and casual *sang-froid*. Or maybe it was the way he ran a gloved hand through his hair, taking it from fashionably tousled to deliciously rumpled.

Mmmmm.

Belle was going to side with the hair. Though sardonic smiles were a close second.

Regardless, her decision to offer marriage to him had not been based on his physical appearance. She was many things, but *flighty* and *shallow* were two words that had never been attached to her.

Replacing his hat, Lord Blake studied her, blue eyes twinkling.

Yes. Definitely amused.

That was . . . encouraging? Having never proposed marriage to a man before, Belle was unsure.

"Enlighten me, if you would be so kind, as to the particular reasons why you think this . . . joint endeavor . . . would be profitable." He gestured toward her.

Oh! Excellent.

That she had come prepared to do.

With a curt nod, she pulled a paper from her reticule.

"A list?" His lips twitched again.

"I am nothing if not thorough in my planning, my lord." She opened the paper with shaking fingers, her hands clammy inside her gloves.

"Of course. I should have expected as much. You arranged this meeting, after all." He tapped the letter in his pocket.

Belle chose to ignore the wry humor in his tone and merely nodded her head in agreement. "Allow me to proceed with my list. Though please forgive me if my reasons appear forward."

"You have just proposed marriage to a peer of the realm, madam. I cannot imagine anything you say from this point onward will trump that."

"True."

A beat.

Lord Blake pinned her with his gaze—calm and guileless. The forthright look of a man who knew himself and would never be less-than-true to his own values.

His gaze upset her breathing, causing something to catch in her throat.

Belle broke eye-contact, swallowing too loudly.

"Allow me to begin." She snapped the paper in her hand. The words swam in her vision, but she knew them by heart. The paper was more for show than anything else. She had done her calculations most carefully.

Taking a fortifying breath, Belle began, "Firstly, you have newly inherited the Marquisate of Blake from a cousin. Your cousin was somewhat imprudent in his spending habits—"

"I would declare the man to be an utter scapegrace and wastrel, but continue."

"Regardless of the cause, your lands and estates are in dire need of resuscitation." Belle glanced at him over the top of her paper. "You are basically without funds, my lord."

"As my solicitor repeatedly reminds me." He shot her an arch look. "It is why I am trying to fund a business venture in connection with the East India Company, as you are also undoubtedly aware."

"Yes, my lord. That is why I am proposing an enterprise of a slightly different sort. Allow me to continue." Belle cleared her throat, looking down to her paper. "My own family is genteel with connections to the upper aristocracy—my great-great grandfather was the Earl of Stratton—though we have no proper title of our own, leaving my father to make his own way in the world. I, as you might already know, am a considerable heiress. My father was a prominent banker and left the entirety of his estate to me upon his death three years past."

Belle clenched her jaw against the familiar sting in her throat.

Blink, blink, blink.

Now was *not* the time to dwell upon her father.

"Are you indeed?" he asked. "Though I do not wish to sound crass, I feel we left polite discussion in the dust several minutes ago, so I must enquire: How much of an heiress are you, precisely?"

Did she hear keen interest in his tone? Or was Lord Blake simply exceedingly polite?

"I believe the current amount stands somewhere in the region of eighty thousand pounds, my lord," she replied.

Lord Blake froze at that staggering number, just as Belle had predicted he would.

"Eighty thousand pounds, you say? That is a dowry of marquess-saving proportions."

"My thoughts precisely, my lord."

Her father had originally left her a healthy sixty thousand pounds, but she was nothing if not her father's daughter. Numbers and statistics flowed through her brain, a constant rushing river. She had used these skills to grow her fortune.

It was what her father would have wanted. Refusing to see her gender as a barrier, her father had taught his only child everything he knew—financial systems, probabilities, market shares—even soliciting her opinions during that last year before his death.

By the age of sixteen, Belle understood more about supply-and-demand and the mathematics of economics than most noblemen. Knowing this, the conditions in her father's will allowed her to continue to oversee her own interests with the help of his solicitor, Mr. Sloan. At only nineteen years of age, she currently managed a thriving financial empire.

She could hear her father's gruff voice, his hand gently lifting her chin. *I would give you choices, my Little Heart Full. A lady should always have options. I would see you happy.*

Belle swallowed back the painful tightness in her throat.

Now, if she could only land a husband and free herself from the guardianship of her uncle and mother.

Family, it turned out, were not quite as simple to manage as corn shares.

Her mother, hungry for a title for her daughter, was becoming increasingly bold in her attempts to get Belle married. She had all but forced Belle to betroth herself to a cold, aloof viscount the previous Season. Fortunately, the viscount—Lord Linwood—had asked to be released from their betrothal.

But the entire situation had left Belle feeling helpless.

She *detested* feeling helpless, she realized. And so she used that unwelcome sensation to suppress her inherent shyness and overcome her retiring personality.

Belle would solve the husband problem herself. She simply needed to reduce the entire situation to a statistical probability and face it as she would any other business transaction.

"Eighty-thousand pounds," Lord Blake repeated. "Are husbands—particularly the marquess variety—generally so costly?" He clasped his hands behind his back, studying her. "I had not thought to price them before this."

"I cannot say. This is my first venture into, uhmm . . ."

"Purchasing a husband?" he supplied, eyes wide.

Heavens. Was that a hint of displeasure creeping into his voice?

"I am not entirely sure I agree with the word *purchase*, my lord—"

"True. It does smack of trade and all polite society knows we cannot have *that*."

A pause.

"Shall we use the word *negotiate* instead?" she asked.

He cocked his head, considering. "I daresay that would be better. So I receive a sultan's ransom and your lovely self, and you receive . . ." His words drifted off.

"A husband. And in the process, I become Lady Blake, a peeress of the realm."

"Are you truly so hungry to be a marchioness? Surely eighty thousand pounds could purchase—forgive me, *negotiate*—the title of duchess." His words so very, very dry.

"I am sure my mother would agree with you, my lord, but I am more interested in finding a balance between title and the proper gentleman." She cleared her throat. "You come highly recommended."

"Do I?" Again, his tone darkly sardonic.

Oh, dear.

But as she was already in for more than a penny, why not aim for the whole pound?

"I did not arrive at the decision to propose marriage lightly. I had my solicitor hire a Runner to investigate you. I have armed myself with information, my lord."

Belle wisely did not add that, after crunching all the statistical probabilities, Lord Blake had been by far and away her preferred candidate. She was quite sure that, like most people, he would not appreciate being reduced to a number.

"Information? About me?" he asked.

"Yes. For example, I know you recently cashed out of the army, selling the officer's commission you inherited from your father. All those who served with you report you to be an honest and worthy commander—"

"As well they should."

"Additionally, you are a kind son to your mother. You send her and your stepfather funds when you are able. You visit regularly. Your four older sisters dote upon you, and you are godfather to at least one of each of their children. You are a tremendous favorite with all of your nieces and nephews. All of this speaks highly to the kind of husband and father you would be."

After her disastrous betrothal to Lord Linwood last year, Belle was determined to not make the same error twice. She learned from her mistakes. Her mother and uncle would not browbeat her into accepting one of their suitors again.

If nothing else, eighty thousand pounds should purchase—*negotiate*—her a *kindhearted* husband of her own choice.

Lord Blake shuffled his feet. "I-I really am at a loss for words, Miss Heartstone. I am trying to decide if I should be flattered or utterly appalled."

Belle sucked in a deep breath, her mouth as dry as the Sahara.

Stay strong. Argue your case.

She pasted a strained smile on her face. "Might I suggest siding with flattery, my lord?"

Visit www.NicholeVan.com to buy your copy of
Seeing Miss Heartstone today and continue the story.

About the Author

THE SHORT VERSION:

NICHOLE VAN IS A WRITER, photographer, designer and generally disorganized crazy person. Though originally from Utah, she currently lives on the coast of Scotland with three similarly crazy children and one sane, very patient husband who puts up with all of them. In her free time, she enjoys long walks along the Scottish lochs and braes. She does not, however, enjoy haggis.

THE LONG OVERACHIEVER VERSION:

AN INTERNATIONAL BESTSELLING AUTHOR, Nichole Van is an artist who feels life is too short to only have one obsession. In former lives, she has been a contemporary dancer, pianist, art historian, choreographer, culinary artist and English professor.

Most notably, however, Nichole is an acclaimed photographer, winning over thirty international accolades for her work, including Portrait of the Year from WPPI in 2007. (Think Oscars for wedding and portrait photographers.) Her unique photography style has been featured in many magazines, including Rangefinder and Professional Photographer. She is also the creative mind behind the popular website Flourish Emporium which provides resources for photographers.

All that said, Nichole has always been a writer at heart. With an MA in English, she taught technical writing at Brigham Young University for ten years and has written more technical manuals than she can quickly count. She decided in late 2013 to start writing fiction and has since become an Amazon #1 bestselling author. Additionally, she has won a RONE award, as well as been a Whitney Award Finalist several years running. Her late 2018 release, *Seeing Miss Heartstone*, won the Whitney Award Winner for Best Historical Romance.

In February 2017, Nichole, her husband and three children moved from the Rocky Mountains in the USA to Scotland. They currently live near the coast of eastern Scotland in an eighteenth-century country house. Nichole loves her pastoral country views while writing and enjoys long walks through fields and along beaches.

She is known as NicholeVan all over the web: Facebook, Instagram, Pinterest, etc. Visit http://www.NicholeVan.com to sign up for her author newsletter and be notified of new book releases.

If you enjoyed this book, please leave a short review on Amazon. com. Wonderful reviews are the elixir of life for authors. Even better than dark chocolate.